ANN DENTON

LE RUE PUBLISHING

Copyright © 2019 Ann Denton

1st Edition

All rights reserved. No part of this publication may be
reproduced, distributed, or transmitted in any form or by
any means, including photocopying, recording, or other
electronic or mechanical methods, without the prior
written permission of the publisher, except in the case of
brief quotations embodied in critical reviews and certain
other noncommercial uses permitted by copyright law.
For permission requests, write to the publisher, addressed
"Attention: Permissions Coordinator," at the address
below.

Le Rue Publishing
320 South Boston Avenue, Suite 1030
Tulsa, OK 74103
www.LeRuePublishing.com

ISBN: 978-1-951714-98-7

To All the Angels Living in Sin...

CHAPTER 1

RUBY

"I FUCKING HATE YOU!" HOLLY SCREAMED AT ME BEFORE she stormed out of the store for the second time this week.

"Hate? Hate? Hold on, let me grab my dictionary for that one." Gah! English. It was the hardest language ever—and I'd learned thirty-five so far, mostly aquatic dialects (which were basically gargling with different intonations).

I flitted over to the cash register in my shoe shop, half-flying, half-skipping because I couldn't let Holly see my wings. I had to hide them with magic.

Holly had said that word with such intensity. It had to be a good one. I dug through the piles of receipts to find the well-worn book that I always kept on-hand at work. But

Holly didn't wait for me to look up the word hate—a word I'd never heard before.

Instead, her blonde, teenage ponytail disappeared out the front door and around the corner of Main Street into the sunset.

I found my dictionary and made my way over to the white leather chairs in the center of my show room. I didn't have any customers today anyway, so I sat down in one of the chairs people normally used to try on shoes and looked up the word. Hat: A shaped covering for the head worn for warmth... that didn't sound right. How could Holly hat me? Ugh. Was this one of those annoying words like knife? With all those letters that didn't need to be there?

I leaned over to the Alexa that Holly had installed for me. "Hey, Alexa, what's hate?"

Alexa responded with: "Hate: intense, passionate dislike."

Could people dislike angels? I looked up at the ceiling. I mean, was *He* gonna let Holly get away with that?

Nothing happened. So, apparently, the answer was yes. People could hate angels.

"Really?" I asked the ceiling. All I'd asked her to do was take out the trash after our newest shoe delivery. But Holly had teared up, her blue eyes welling, before she screamed that word hate and stomped out. Did trash make her sad? Was it a phobia? Or were those angry tears? I'd read about those. Angry-crying was a thing.

I sighed. There were just too many options. Humans cried when they were happy, sad, even angry. How were you supposed to tell?

And nothing in *Harmony's Guide to Humans* said anything about humans hating trash.

I pulled off my flats and dug my toes into my plush white rug in the middle of my showroom for a second. I had white couches and chairs for customers who tried on the shoes I sourced from around the world. Behind me, on the white wall, adorable little shoe display cubbies were lit with the light from heaven—electricity was far too expensive since I only sold shoes every few days. Next to me, a cardboard tower of brand-new shoe boxes stood like little presents just waiting to be opened. How could anyone be mad in here? Or feel hate?

It shouldn't be possible, I thought, before opening up a couple of new shoe boxes and pulling out the softest shoes I could find. I caressed them before I slipped them onto my feet. They were Tree Loungers and the box said their color was fog, though, having been raised in the clouds, I considered myself an expert on condensation. This was more of a sooty ash color. The manufacturers got it wrong. As humans so often did.

I took a test step off my rug and onto the hard cement floor to try out my newest product. I leaned over to look at them as I walked. Decent. Not cloud-level comfort, that was certain, but the shoes had arch support and no heel. I had to flutter my wings a bit to keep from tunking over face first, because this gravity stuff was a total downer.

Earth had far more gravity than heaven or any of the planets I'd been stationed on before.

I didn't get how other angels did it. I'd been here just over a year and the balance thing still got to me. I'd petitioned for smaller boobs, thinking the frontal weight might be causing the issue, but the Mortal Bodies Commission was all wrapped up in some hearing because someone added a tentacle where they weren't supposed to. So, who knew when I'd hear back about the boob reduction.

I sighed, stopped walking, and stared at the trash bag in front of me. My thoughts went back to Holly. She'd been fine three minutes ago. I squinted at the trash bag, trying to decide if it looked like some evil earth creature and that's why Holly had gone bonkers. I crouched in front of the bag and poked at it. To me, it just looked like a shiny boulder. But maybe she had a fear of boulders?

"Hey Alexa, are people scared of rocks?"

Alexa started to list off types of rocks, completely ignoring my question.

Suddenly, a ball of light appeared in front of me, hovering just at eye level. I squinted, blinded by the intensity of the bright white orb. It was like a miniature sun, only lacking the heat. "Stars, Gunther! Do you have to be so bright?"

My supervisor's laugh drifted over me. But he dimmed a little as he bounced up and down in front of me. "It's the fastest way to show up on this planet," he replied.

I fought against rolling my eyes. A witch named Amethyst

had taught me that habit—humans did it to show they were annoyed. But I didn't think my supervisor would appreciate it. So, I smiled instead. "How can I help you?"

"Just checking in on your progress. Miracle by Christmas still on track?" Gunther asked.

"The girl's working here," I responded with a noncommittal shrug. Creating this store and then convincing the teenager she needed a job here had taken three months. But changing her rotten attitude? Helping her regain the faith? It was mid-November. The chances of me pulling this off by Christmas hovered somewhere between the chance of being struck by lightning and the chance of winning the lottery—which according to the guy at the gas station who explained the ticket to me, was none. "I could really use a better guide on human emotions—" *Because they make no thundering sense!*

A scroll shot out of the ball of light and smacked me in the chest. "Ow!"

I rubbed at the sore spot as I bent to pick the scroll up off the floor. I nearly fell but tossed my wings out to help regain my balance. The scroll was thick, probably a foot in circumference. I peeled it open and read, "Harmony's Guide to Humans: The Teenage Years: An Instruction Manual." I glazed over all the formal text to find the publication date. "1745." I sighed. "Why haven't we updated this thing?"

Gunther's orb of light bounced up off the ceiling and then off the floor before floating aimlessly around my shoe shop. "Red tape. It takes the Committee on Humanity centuries to approve updates. Just know, the dueling section is definitely obsolete. The guide to marriage is only applicable in some countries. But the section on STDs? You're gonna want to check that out."

"Well, the Committee might want to get a move on. The other guide I've been using obviously didn't work out."

A snort came from the ball of light, and little sparks shot out across the room.

"Look, Gunther, we all know that last year … didn't go well." That was the understatement of the year. Last Christmas, my attempt at a miracle had been a disaster. A disaster that had made me the laughingstock of heaven.

I fingered my little wings. They'd been shrunk into tiny, two-feather horrors as a consequence of my failure to pull off a miracle for George Barley. They could hardly be called wings anymore. They looked awful, like baby cupid wings, but didn't even work as well as those. I glanced over at my boss, who was lazily spinning in midair, changing colors like some DJ party light. "Don't you think I could transfer back to the warrior division?" I crossed my fingers as I asked.

Those were the good days. You saw a demon, you killed it. Or you helped your warriors—aka the good guys—kill the demon's warriors—aka the bad guys. It was all very cut and dry. Good and evil. Alive and dead.

This miracle stuff was the pits. Humans were so emotional. About everything. Even trash, apparently.

Gunther made his edges waver. "No can do. Everyone has to do a miracle rotation. Cheer up, kid. You've only got ninety-nine years to go!"

I swallowed a groan as Gunther circled me.

"Unless you mess up again, of course," he added. "Three strikes and you're done."

My stomach curdled like cottage cheese—that disgusting substance Holly constantly shoved down her throat that looked like clotted alien jizz.

"I'm gonna send you a mentor, someone to help you out," his voice wrapped around me.

His words were supposed to be comforting but panic shot down my spine. I didn't want a mentor. I didn't need someone breathing down my neck, telling me how to put one foot in front of the other. I'd made one mistake, for cloud's sake! "What I need is a better guide to humans."

"You're getting a personal guide."

"But—"

"No buts. You know the three strikes rule. You've had one. The second isn't looking good. I don't want you to get it. Because angels who get a second strike nearly always get a third."

I swallowed hard. "Yeah," I said quietly. And if I got a third

… I'd get transferred. Downstairs. As in … I'd have to live in the nether regions. I shuddered. I did not want to become a demon. That was the worst fate an angel could have. To be sent to the dark side.

"Now, go find your target and get a move on. Your mentor will get here tomorrow. Peace out!" Gunther chuckled as his ball of light shrunk to a pinprick and then popped into nothingness.

Great. Just great. I have an impossible mission and now a mentor to hide from.

In heaven, a mentor was the equivalent of what Amethyst called a micro-manager, a control freak, like her ex. Angels had great intentions. Always. But execution … yeah, sometimes we weren't the best at that. Probably because we were so rolled up in rules, and our lack of free will and all. Sometimes being an angel felt like tiptoeing through the fog over thorny thistles. One wrong step and wham! Your poor toesies were ripped to shreds. Mentors meant double the rules. Double the tiptoeing. I had a new word for how I felt about mentors: hate.

I shook my head as I set the scroll down on the ground and took out the garbage myself, rounding the brick corner of my building and mulling over Holly and her insane teenage mood swings. The Committee on Humanity always insisted that emotions were what made humans special. Holly's older sister had taught me the word "special" could have multiple meanings. It made me wonder if the committee was using the other definition. Because Holly was a whack job.

I blew a raspberry at the trash bag, grumbling, "Warrior angels have it so easy." I stared at the black plastic and reminisced wistfully about my days in sector seventeen, on the various planets there. Back when my wings were the size of my entire body.

I glanced around the alley. No humans were around. There was only a cute little bunny shifter hopping around a couple doors down. But supernaturals were all aware of one another. They knew I existed. So I didn't have to pretend to be human around them. Thank goodness. I used my wings to hover so I could throw the bag full of cardboard into the giant green dumpster. But my ridiculous wings were far too small for my body weight unless I flapped at awful hummingbird speeds. What should have been a hover was more of an awkward, prolonged jump. When I landed, my foot touched a puddle of goop. Nasty, sticky brown goop that smelled like sewage.

Thunderheads! That was the second pair of shoes I'd ruined this week!

I stomped back to my shop and tossed out the shoes. I went to the bathroom in the back and cleaned my feet, grumpy that Holly hadn't done her job, grumpy about my dirty foot, grumpy that I was getting a mentor and had another century to go in the miracle division. A century on earth! How was I ever gonna stand it?

Killing bad guys! Easy peasy. But how the *bad place* was I supposed to take someone who'd lost faith and restore it?

You'd think appearing to them would do it. Poof. I'm an angel. Angels exist. God exists. Believe! Be good!

But no. Humans were so stubbornly illogical. They adored things that made zero sense at all. Like kittens. "Hello, small furry creature who cannot stand the sight of me. I'm going to embrace and caress you against your will." WHAT? The Earthly Critter Committee kept advising God to give cats bigger claws in order to protect themselves against this atrocity, but he hadn't consented yet. For some reason, he found humanity's logical fallacies amusing. And humans lived with emotions going haywire. Just like Holly.

I kicked the new scroll, watching it unravel until it met my shaggy white rug. I wouldn't find anything useful in there; no women's rights, Instagram selfies, or blenders—which I had completely thought were the devil's evil invention until Holly introduced me to a smoothie. *Mixed berry with energy infusion—now that's angelic inspiration at work, right there.*

My stomach grumbled. That was the one good part about becoming corporeal over the past year. Eating.

I made myself a smoothie and locked up The Perfect Fit early. It wasn't like I had customers anyway. I made my way to the graveyard as darkness fell, determined to find Holly's big sister. I'd have her help me get a plan together for this miracle before my mentor showed up tomorrow and started trying to boss me around. Operation Miracle ASAP was about to commence.

The cemetery gate creaked as I pushed it open.

"Those hooligans are at it again!" Muriel whooshed toward me; her ghostly, semi-transparent face contorted in fury as her giant old-fashioned plumed hat flew off her head. She pointed a gnarled, accusing finger back behind the big crypt. Silver Springs Cemetery wasn't that big, because the town wasn't that big. There was only one crypt; it belonged to the ice-cream barons of upstate New York, the Weatherhouser family.

"What?" I nearly dropped my smoothie.

"They are face-making over there." Muriel's tone was pure disgust as she picked at the buttons of the prim, high-collared dress she'd died in.

I set down my smoothie on a gravestone and started to flutter my wings, letting my feet hover a few inches off the ground. I pulled my waist-length brown hair up into a ponytail as I cocked my head. "Face-making? Are you sure?" I mean, this was His favorite planet. But really? I stared at Muriel's grey eyes. "God sometimes gives seminars on making faces and bodies from clay, but I've never gotten to go to one."

Her jaw dropped. That meant awe, right? I was pretty certain *Harmony* had covered that in the chapter on human expressions. Awe was the exact right emotion for this. Watching God create new life was supposed to be awesome. "I've heard it's amazing. He takes this ball of dust—oohh, I wanna see!" I clapped, excited. Finally, something cool happening on this planet! I turned to look at the crypt, which had a giant flying horse carved on the side.

Muriel's cold, see-through arm latched onto mine. Her wrinkles were edged in white as she leaned her face closer to mine. "Trust me, you don't want to see. They are *basket-weaving.*"

Sometimes Muriel liked to overemphasize her words in weird ways. And mix her metaphors. I arched an eyebrow. "I thought you said they were making faces." Disappointment ran through me. Of course, it was too good to be true. God wasn't down here. He wasn't giving demonstrations. I sighed. I hadn't heard of ghosts with memory problems before, but I supposed it was a possibility. Silver Springs was a bit different than most towns with its large supernatural population. So, maybe Muriel was a bit different than most ghosts. Or maybe the fact that she'd been a ghost since 1902 might have been part of it. Maybe that was too long of a ghost-life?

Muriel put a hand to her forehead as though I was giving her a headache. "Don't you know any of the sayings for …" She leaned in and whispered, "Amorous congress?"

"I thought this country had Congress in a different state." I was pretty sure I read that somewhere. But so many dimensions, so many planets, so many rules … after a while it was hard to tell. But even if I wasn't certain where Congress was, I was certain that Muriel was losing it. She had jumped topics three sentences in a row. Maybe she needed my miracle-working, not Holly. Though Muriel swore she wouldn't cross over until one of her descendants became President. Maybe the Congress thing was a delusion.

Muriel let out a sound that was nearly a growl. She was such a grumpy ghost. She almost made it a bummer for me to hang out in the cemetery. Luckily, Maddie was a young ghost—and the reason I still regularly visited.

Maddie was super helpful, telling me all about humans and life on earth and all the weird little quirks that you didn't hear about when you were just working day in and day out for the Man. Like, she taught me that men who wear plaid can't be trusted. I had no idea that was even a thing! Wish I'd known that last year, before the miracle debacle. I'd have thunk twice before trying to help that old crankpot, George. He was a plaid-wearer.

Maddie was wise beyond the twenty-years she'd been alive before she'd choked on a grape and become a ghost. She also happened to be Holly's sister. She'd helped me choose her sister as this year's miracle target. And she was the reason I was here tonight. If anyone would know how to calm down Holly and get her back on track, it would be Maddie. I summoned her. "Maddie!"

Maddie materialized just beside Muriel. She was a ghost with a diamond in her nose, half her head shaved, the other half had shoulder-length semi-transparent hair Maddie swore was rainbow-colored when she was alive, before it turned the universal undead white. She took one look at the angry old ghost and immediately knew what was going on. "Stop ruining everybody's fun." Maddie shot a big jet of air at Muriel—blowing the other ghost halfway across the cemetery. Muriel's howl convinced a couple walking down the street to clutch each other close and hurry past in the darkness.

"You could be a bit nicer," I gently scolded. If Maddie would just tone it down a bit, I was certain she could cross over to the good side. But she was constantly making choices that kept her here. Sometimes I wondered if it was on purpose, if she was sticking around for Holly. But I didn't press. It was against Hallelujah Code 4.48-72 - Free Choice. People had to make their own decisions. Including ghosts.

Maddie just blew a raspberry at me.

I sighed. "I think Muriel's gone crazy. She's saying nonsense things are happening over here."

I started to fly off in the direction Muriel had indicated all the mystery activity was occurring, behind the crypt. Face-making, basket-weaving, Congress? Her sayings were so crazy, I just had to find out what the fuss was all about. I circled around the edge of the crypt, hovering with my wings just a few feet in the air so that my feet wouldn't crunch through any of the crisp November leaves. It was hard work—exhausting—but those leaves could be awfully sharp and poky. And they hid evil sticks underneath them. Walking on earth was nowhere near as good as walking on heaven's clouds. It was darn near dangerous, what with potholes and black ice and all the uneven awfulness. It was why I'd settled on a shoe store. People needed foot protection. I took a deep breath to get my mind off the ground and back into curious mode before I peeked around the corner of the crypt.

What I saw had *nothing* to do with baskets. I saw a very beautiful—very naked—vampire woman straddling a nude young man. She bent over his neck, licking up blood from a bite she'd already made, as her hips shifted back and forth on top of him.

Hmmm… my head tilted as I wondered briefly why the cloud Muriel wouldn't just say there was a mating ritual going on behind the crypt.

Next to me, Maddie's hand pinched her own semi-trans-parent nipple through her shirt while she watched. "Super-hot, huh?" she whispered.

I wasn't sure what she meant. The weather was actually quite brisk. But then, as the dark-haired vampire woman leaned back and moaned in pleasure, I felt a tightening sensation in my abdomen and the space between my thighs heated. Was that what Maddie meant by hot? Did humans have internal heat? This corporeal body was so different from what I was used to. Aquatic bodies were usually cold-blooded, not warm-blooded like this.

Yet another detail lacking from the manual.

I watched the vampire's breasts bounce up and down as she rode her mate. Maddie might be an expert on human things, but breasts were something I knew all about. I leaned over toward Maddie and whispered back, "We've done various angelic studies in different realms. Apparently, gelatinous substances are *always* attractive. That's why God made boobs jiggle."

Next to me, Maddie burst into laughter. I wasn't sure why bouncing breasts were funny to her. That was counter to all the research I'd ever read about them being erogenous. I debated telling my brother, who was on the Universal Reproductive Committee. But that would involve a trip back to heaven. And that was not gonna happen until my wings got bigger. No way I was gonna let him call me a parakeet again. That was a humiliation I'd only suffer once in eternity, thank you.

The vampire turned to glare at us even as she swiveled her hips. "If you're going to ruin the mood, get out."

"Sapphire—" the man started to gulp air. His face turned slightly red.

Sapphire just shushed him and scolded us, "Look, either join us or go the fuck away. Shouldn't you be RIP and all that?"

Maddie clapped back. "There ain't no resting in peace here. You picked the wrong cemetery for that."

She held her hand up for a high five. I didn't really understand, but she'd taught me never to 'leave her hanging' so I smacked her smoky hand. Though I was an angel, the ability to physically interact with ghosts was supposed to be a perk. Something about exorcisms or whatnot. I hadn't bothered to read up on that yet. That was level five stuff.

Below us, in the dull brown grass, the man's hand flew to his nose. He clamped down on his face and wiggled under the vampire, who set her hand on his chest to make him grow still. But he couldn't hold it in. The man inhaled hard. And then, he sneezed. Suddenly, he shifted into a pegasus. A pegasus on his back, wings spread on the grass, belly up and hooves awkwardly waving in the air. Because he was still connected to his mate.

The vampire screeched.

Maddie immediately clamped her hands over her eyes. "OMG. Ew!"

I tilted my head and looked at my ghost friend. "What's wrong?"

She didn't answer. She disappeared. I wondered if, before she'd died, Maddie had never seen any interspecies mating. I sighed. Was that not a thing on Earth? *Harmony's Guide* said nothing about it.

But they "petted" cats. Clearly, humans were attracted to other species.

My hands clenched as I flew off to find Maddie. I needed answers. And I needed to tell her about what a brat her little sister Holly was being. Because I was either gonna get this thundering miracle right or I was going to have to find a new one. I was not going through another Christmas like last year. I was not gonna get another strike. This year, I was gonna get my miracle right.

CHAPTER 2

Barrister

"Blasphemy! That's such bullshit! You know DC characters are one dimensional!" Miguel slammed his hand down on the table. One of his Infinity Gems popped off his costume and rolled away.

"Dude, calm down, Migs," I told Miguel, scratching at my stomach where my stuffed Pikachu kept rubbing against my abs. I'd left my shirt unbuttoned on my Ash Ketchum costume—my last minute, embarrassing-as-hell, piece of crap cosplay costume because my ex had "picked up" my custom Rocket Racoon costume from the tailor and stolen it. The stupid Pika I'd bought online was made of sandpaper, apparently. I pulled him off the velcro strip I'd attached to my jeans and moved him to my shoulder, trading out Bulbasaur. Then I adjusted my red and white ball cap and smiled apologetically at a woman dressed as Storm from X-Men nearby.

People in fantastic costumes roamed around the room, coming and going through the open door to the big hall that was lined with booths and vendors. The smell of churros drifted through the door and my stomach grumbled. For one day, City Hall's Convention Center had been transformed from a dull place for business meetings into a grown-up play place. The local Silver Springs Cosplay Celebration was an annual event. Normally, it was *the* annual event for my friends and I to nerd out and hook up with hot, geeky girls who drove up from nearby towns and celebrate our awesome like-minded addictions. I'd camped overnight last night and gotten fourteen signatures today, from Aquaman to the actor that played my favorite Soul Reaper in the anime *Bleach*. It had been a good day. But our friend Brad had bought a table at the convention and apparently was using it just to piss off Migs. I rolled my eyes. Brad was such a dick—always harassing Migs about something.

Miguel shook his head and pulled off his blue-grey Thanos mask as he crouched down to search for his missing gem. He swiped some sweat off his brow since he'd picked a costume that was basically the equivalent of a space heater. Then he scratched at the scruff he never grew into a full beard. His Spanish accent came out as he growled, "No, I'm not gonna calm down. He knows Marvel is better than DC. Boludo Brad frickin' knows it. He's saying this shit to get under my skin." His blue eyes rolled in their sockets as Brad—up at a podium—said some other stupid shit, and then Migs full-on crawled under the table. He was seriously the weirdest, whitest looking Argentinian dude I'd ever met. His temper flared white-hot over the dumbest shit sometimes though.

Brad kept talking over Miguel's search, going on about how Wonder Woman was created to inspire women during World War II. I disagreed, but the dude had paid to have a table and present, so whatever. We could just walk away from his nonsense.

Migs kept searching for his stone as I glanced around the room, doing one of those awkward apologetic shrugs. If Miguel kept on like this, there was zero chance in hell that the Harley Quinn cougar who'd been eyeing him all night would bite. Right now, she was shaking her head and tugging her friend in the opposite direction.

Miguel might have looked like a model with his stupid square jaw and shit. But his mouth. Dammit all. He was so stubbornly logical and so utterly determined he was right. About everything. So, if his Thanos costume—one of the most hated super villains ever—didn't cock block him, his yelling was about to do the job.

Brad said, "Batman is a better vigilante than any of Avengers."

"That's a lie!" Miguel bumped his head on the table as he argued. "Daredevil is as much a vigilante as Batman."

Shit. I took off my ballcap and swiped at the sweat beading on my own brow. But mine wasn't from a hot costume, it was from nerves. I didn't have a silver tongue like our friend Parker, or crazy good looks like Migs. I worked out like crazy to move myself up from guy-next-door to hot. But that meant I didn't get easy outs like my two best friends. People didn't just excuse me for being a dick. And right now, I was getting all the stink eye that people would never direct at Migs.

I leaned under the table and whisper-growled, "Leave the gem and let's just go somewhere else. It looks like the line for DJ Qualls is pretty short." That last bit was a complete lie, but I was desperate to get him out of here. I saw someone talking to security in the distance and even though it was a bit paranoid of me, I couldn't help but wonder if they were complaining about us.

Crap.

"Come on, man." I urged him.

Migs shook his head. "No. I sold a bit of my soul for this —" he swiped his fingers underneath a cardboard display and all I could do was cross my fingers and hope he didn't dick it up.

He came up clutching a red-orange soul stone that glowed a tiny bit purple around the edges.

"Ha-ha," I fake laughed at him. "I get it. Soul stone. Sold your soul. Good one. Okay, let's go." I sat back in my chair and gathered my stuff as he crawled out from under the table.

Miguel grinned, his blue eyes sparkling as I led him out of

the room. He turned and flipped Brad off one last time before the door closed behind us. Then he said, "Oh no, man. It gets better. I'm not even joking. All these stones? I traded them to this hippie chick, Wiccan or something; she works at that Hex You shop." He threw his head back and laughed as he replaced the stone in the gauntlet on his left hand. "That woman literally gave me the stones for free. All I had to do was sign a little piece of paper telling her I granted her a bit of my soul." He threw his head back and laughed. "Crazy right?"

Cold fear slid down my spine. "What?" I tried not to sound panicked. But I was fucking panicked. "What was her name?"

"Amy? No. Amethyst? I dunno man."

I tried not to hyperventilate. Migs traded part of his soul? And he didn't even know who had it?

This was bad. I should know. I'd traded away a bit of my soul once. And while I'd do it again … I'd known who I was selling it to and what I was getting for it.

Migs … damn. He didn't believe. But shit. Souls were real. This shit was real. And it could get real bad real fast.

I slipped my phone out of my pocket and unlocked it. I needed to text Parker ASAP.

Miguel waved a hand casually. "Yeah, I looked at stones like these online, dude. Crazy. There's a set on eBay for like $180.00. I offered to trade the woman some unicorn farts if she had any diamonds, but she didn't take me up on it." He guffawed, completely amused by himself. Completely unaware that all the blood had fled from my face.

Shit.

My best friend had just sold part of his soul to a witch and then mocked her?

I texted Parker, our business partner and a local tech demon. A demon that Migs thought was just human. Because he didn't know about the things that went bump in the night. Didn't believe in them.

SOS

Really? I'm screwing up a server down in NYC right now.

Yes. Soul-binding issues.

BRT

I breathed a sigh of relief as we moved into the larger part of City Hall that was set up with displays for different handmade arts and crafts. Some woman with knitted toilet cozies that looked like shields tried to wave us over, but I steered Miguel toward the food.

Maybe if I shoved a hot dog in his face, he'd calm down and we could wait it out until Parker came and helped me track down the bitch who'd taken Mig's soul. I made him sit and grabbed him food as a few of our friends wandered over to join us.

"Dude, you get less action than my grandma's backdoor!"

Brad snorted at our friend Dez as they both took seats next to Migs. Dammit, we hadn't escaped him. He must have wrapped up his presentation as soon as Migs stopped arguing with him.

"I know your grandma," Dez said. "Almost asked her to be my Yzma." Dez did finger guns in his Disney Kuzco costume. It was the lamest thing I'd ever seen—who even remembered *The Emperor's New Groove*? But somehow, he pulled it off, even though he wore a woman's wig and a damn skirt.

I nudged Miguel with my elbow since I had two hotdogs in hand. "Mustard and onions?"

Migs gave me a nod and I started fixing his dog.

Brad gestured at me as I handed over the hotdog "Dude, you're whipped. If you two start making out, I'm leaving."

I flipped Brad off.

Miguel simply corrected him. "We're hetero life mates. Look it up."

Brad curled his lip.

But Dez held up a hand. "Do not be bagging on the wisdom of Jay and Silent Bob. Hetero life mates are a thing, dude. You know it."

Brad rolled his eyes and left the table to grab a drink and start putting the moves on a curvy version of Poison Ivy.

I sat down next to Miguel, and dug in. Cheap, fatty hot

dog grease ran down my lip.

And that was the moment my ex walked up. Darlene.

And fuck me if she wasn't dressed like a goddamned sexy Pikachu. *How the fuck had she known I was dressing up as Ash from Pokemon?* I wondered as I smeared the grease around on my chin with a cheap paper napkin. *Probably that idiot, Brad. He'd have thought it was funny.*

Even thinking about her got me half-hard. Which pissed me the fuck off. Darlene was a cheating bitch. And a costume thief.

I tried to shove the memories of her away. It had been almost six months. I should be over it by now.

I turned and gave her half my back, real mature-like. But I didn't give a damn.

Migs had my back, like always. Fucking bro was the best. "Get outta here before I call the cops and tell them you stole his suit," he growled at her.

"I just want to talk—"

I stood up, suddenly not at all interested in my hot dog. I tossed it in the trash and walked in the other direction.

Migs had a few words with my ex before he caught up with me standing near a Mercs costume club table. Two hot chicks sat at the table, and a line of guys were waiting to sign up.

To distract myself, I tossed my arm around Miguel's

shoulder. "Betcha I could hook you up with one of the girls up ahead. Which one you want?"

He sighed and shrugged me off. "Not gonna happen. Waste of time."

"It might not be."

"The last four girls you've tried to hook me up with have had serious issues."

"Just because they didn't know much about video games—"

"Or politics, or physics, or common sense—" Migs added. "No. Seriously. Besides, look how messed up you still are about Darlene. I don't need that. I'm good."

I was gonna argue that the dude went through more pocket pussies than an adult toy store, but he pushed through the doors that led outside.

"I'm going home, man," Migs said. He gave me the nod and started to walk off.

I stood there, under the harvest moon on the steps of City Hall, debating if I wanted to follow him. Part of me wanted to go home. But the other part wanted a fucking drink. Maybe five. Why the hell did Darlene have to show up? And where the hell was Parker? We needed to do something about Migs. My best friend didn't know it, but demons were real. Souls were real. And atheist Migs had unknowingly traded away something he really shouldn't have. To some stranger!

I rubbed my forehead in frustration as I wondered what the fuck I was gonna do. I walked over to Main Street. Problems like this definitely called for alcohol.

I hurried past the graveyard; for some reason, it gave me the creeps. Maybe knowing demons were real had just made me more freaked out about everything.

Up ahead, some other people in costumes were obviously doing what I was. Heading to Vee, the "it" place in Silver Springs to go clubbing. They were parting and walking around something—I hoped there wasn't some weirdo passed out in the road. I grabbed my phone in case I needed to call Parker.

But there wasn't a drunk passed out on the sidewalk.

When the crowd parted, I swear my heart stopped.

Standing there on the cobblestones, looking like the innocent picture of every wet dream I'd ever had, was an angel.

A literal angel. Complete in a cosplay costume that was one of the most perfect I'd ever seen.

Holy motherfucking shit, this girl was fine. How had I missed her at the convention? She didn't look like any character I recognized. This girl looked like a fucking Victoria Secret model—wings and all. Except she wore a cute, conservative but form-fitting little white dress that stopped just above her knees, instead of just a bra and panties. Thank God. Otherwise, I might have to punch out the Captain America who turned around to check out her ass.

My eyes scanned her from top to bottom. This woman had dark brown hair, so dark it almost looked black. It fell in waves that caressed her breasts, which drew my eyes. I'd always been a breast guy. But then I glanced back up at her face. It was like getting smacked by a two by four. She had grey eyes and these pouty lips that I just *needed* to bite.

Fuck, but the expression on her face. It was so perfect. So sweet and sad. I wanted to gather her into my arms and just—I don't even fucking know—protect her. She had these cute little wings on her costume. And they looked so real, too. They must have been hella expensive. They looked soft. I immediately pictured her riding me, naked except for the wings.

I had to adjust my jeans.

What was wrong with me? I hadn't had thoughts like this since Darlene.

Shit.

Nope. Not going there. Not gonna let some physical reaction to some woman throw me into misery again.

I walked forward steadily, determined to do just a polite nod and be on my way, despite my dick heavily protesting that option. Pick-up lines ran through my head. But I tossed them aside. I was not gonna hit on this girl. I was not gonna use the line I'd tried earlier tonight: "Hey baby,

I wanna Squirtle on your JigglyPuffs." I was gonna walk past and that was that.

But then she started crying.

And fuck me. My mother would fucking kill me dead if I just walked past a woman crying in the street in the middle of the night. Or ever. I took a second glance at the angel. She didn't seem to have a purse. Shit—I realized she didn't even have on real shoes. She wore some kind of soft slippers that made me think of bedrooms. Her. In my bedroom. Shit. Fuck. Focus.

She turned and walked down the street.

Like a creeper, I followed.

I scanned Main Street as she started down it. Had some fuckwad dropped her off? Had her boyfriend just left her like this? A gorilla pounded inside my chest, fucking furious. I had to force him down and swallow before I could walk up to her and ask, "Miss, do you need some help?"

She looked up at me. She blinked those big doe eyes. And I swear if she'd been a semi-truck barreling towards on me, I would have just stood there and let her mow me down. I was *captivated*.

"Um, help. Oh, yes. Maybe. That might be good." She dabbed at her eyes and then stared at the tears on her hands.

Was she in shock? Shit. I didn't know jack about first aid. "Do you need my phone to call someone?" I asked, reaching into my back pocket. As I did, my shirt rubbed against my abs. They were cold. And that's when I realized this woman must be freezing. Girls were always cold right? My mom was.

I yanked my shirt off and handed it to her. "Here. Put this on."

Those wings were even more expensive than I thought, because this woman retracted them. I didn't even see her remote control. Shit, she must be a die hard cosplay fan like me. That thought alone got me breathing hard again. Hot nerd? God, yes. Not to mention the sight of her swallowed up by my shirt. The gorilla in my chest pounded against my ribs, growling that we should claim her.

But I just handed over my phone, electricity shooting up my arm when our fingers touched. I had to tamp down on a nervous laugh.

"Sorry," she muttered, I guess about shocking me. I didn't mind. Not at all.

But then she stared at the phone for a second. Like she wasn't quite certain what to do. "I'm sorry," she handed the phone back to me. "You clearly have a beautiful soul, but I just don't know what to—"

The sound of glass breaking hit our ears, startling me. I turned to look. It was coming from a shoe store.

A shadow moved inside.

Shit!

My blood started pounding and I let that angry gorilla loose. He insisted I move between this woman and the shop. I took a step forward to block her with my body. My skin felt every pinprick of cold. My senses went on high alert. We were witnessing a robbery.

I reached for my phone as the figure inside flipped on a flashlight, revealing a chunk of her face.

Her.

The robber was a woman.

The woman in the angel costume sighed. "Holly." She stepped around me.

I freaked. I put out my hand to block her. Was she insane? You couldn't walk into a break in! Who knew what kind of weapons the person inside had? "What are you doing?" I growled.

"I'm going to go see what's wrong with her."

I grabbed the angel's hand. And even though she was freezing, and I was freezing, when I touched her, I didn't notice the cold anymore. Every part of me zeroed in on her. She had to listen. I had to make her understand. This was crazy-ass dangerous. And I'd just met her. But she was gonna get hurt, so I had to stop her. "You can't do that," I warned her. "We should stay out here and call the police."

"The police? Oh, right. Humans do that."

Whoa. What? If she'd have used a dump truck and poured

ice down my back, I'd have been less surprised. Electric realization buzzed through my veins as I realized I wasn't talking to a girl from the Cosplay Convention. I took a step away. I was talking to an angel. A real angel. I'd fantasized about fucking a heavenly being.

Me—someone who'd traded part of his soul to a demon.

Shit.

I dropped her hand like a hot potato.

"I'm sorry!" I didn't know what to do. Should I bow? Prayer hands? Shit—could angels read minds? I looked up, checking the sky for lightning bolts.

The angel just smiled at me and said, "It's alright. Everything's alright."

Was she talking to me? Was she reassuring me? Because she could read my mind?! Dumb fuck that I was, my hands flew to my head. Like that would stop my thoughts from leaving it.

The angel turned back to the shoe store and tilted her head, exposing a long expanse of graceful neck. "I think Holly's just having a meltdown. Again."

Another crash resounded.

"Who's Holly?" I protested. Angel or not, someone was trashing that store.

"My targe—My employee," she sighed.

That was her store? The angel owned a shoe store? Why

the fuck not—I guess, technically, Miguel and I had a demon for a partner, though he didn't know it. But an employee trashing the angel's place? Bullshit. She had to be the nicest boss ever—probably a pushover, being an angel and all.

"Whoever's in there ain't an employee anymore," I shook my head and unlocked my phone. "I'm calling the cops. That's vandalism." But I paused with the phone halfway to my ear. "Holly isn't a werewolf or anything, right?"

Maybe I should dial Parker instead. He was only a tech demon—so he said. He couldn't rain down hellfire or anything. He could only take out every phone in the tri-state area. But he always "knew a guy."

The angel smiled, and I swear it sent a shaft of light right through me, warming me up. My dick perked up and I had to look away.

Don't think about her boobs. She's a fucking angel. Don't think about them.

The angel sighed and pulled off my shirt, handing it back to me. "This might be my chance to change things. I better go take care of her," her voice had this soft, breathy calm tone. Like this was no big deal.

I shook my head. If someone trashed my store, I'd rend them limb from limb. Or, at least, I'd rip them a new one on social media while Parker had his guys do their thing and never ever told me the details.

"I'm Ruby, by the way," the angel said. "And thank you for

34

offering to help. It was amazing. Very brave of you, considering you're human and you know about were-wolves. You'd make an excellent warrior." And then, the most gorgeous woman—celestial being—I'd ever seen, fluttered her wings and flew off over the top of the building. I guess she was gonna go through the back door. Unlock it and surprise the person inside. Because she was brave. The most perfect woman I'd ever met, and she'd just flown off.

Of course, she did. And I let her. I wasn't sure if it was because Miguel's awkward silence had rubbed off on me. Or because I knew Parker was a demon and he handled shit just fine. Ruby was an angel. A real-life fucking angel. She could handle this.

But I didn't leave. I stayed rooted to the spot. Not because I was creeping. I mean, what if Ruby got attacked? She might need backup. I scanned the road for something I could use to break a window. There was a fallen tree branch nearby, so I scooped that up.

My heart thrummed. I'd never been in a fight before. What if Ruby was wrong? What if that girl Holly wasn't alone in there? What if she'd brought friends? She'd said I'd make a great warrior.

My heart lifted but my brain bitch-slapped it back into place. I was only a warrior in World of Warcraft.

I stared at the store, which started to glow with golden, shimmering light out of nowhere. It sure didn't come from the light bulbs.

The crashing stopped and, as my eyes adjusted to the bright light, I saw Ruby hug a blonde girl. They sank down on this plush white rug.

The girl started crying in Ruby's arms.

Guess she didn't need back up.

I tossed my branch aside. The wind picked up and I buttoned my shirt, getting a little whiff of cinnamon. I pulled my shirt up to my nose and inhaled. Ruby smelled like cinnamon rolls—sugary, sweet goodness.

Fuck.

I looked up at the sky. It was probably sacrilege, but I wished God had let me play the hero. Just this once.

But then a gust of wind blew past me. A tall, pale man with black hipster glasses materialized at my side. "Parker," I said.

The tech demon I'd traded my soul to looked me over and said, "So, what's up?"

I swallowed hard and turned away from Ruby and The Perfect Fit. Because she was perfect, and I was tainted by a deal with a demon.

I would never deserve a woman, let alone an angel, like that.

But I could make damn sure Migs didn't suffer the same fate.

CHAPTER 3

RUBY

HOLLY CRIED IN MY ARMS FOR HOURS AS I HELD HER AND rocked her, huddled on the plush, furry white rug of my showroom. I dimmed the light of heaven so strangers couldn't see in. I decided Holly would want privacy. So I held her in the dark

"I'm sorry, Ruby. I just got so mad," she whimpered. "So fucking mad."

"Shh," I caressed her hair. I kissed the top of her head, like I'd seen parents do to kids on billboards. After I did it, I waited to see if she'd react—get angry or offended or something—but she just clung to my arm and hiccuped. I knew not to mention people's smells (learned that the hard way after I told a woman she smelled like she'd been working outside for three days) but Holly didn't smell good. She smelled like that bottle of Robitussin that Amethyst gave me when I caught a cold a few weeks ago. Like that, but sweeter. The smell leaked from her pores and breath and surrounded us. Part of me worried that Holly's body was broken after she'd drunk that much cough medicine. The other part of me saw the tears leaking from her eyes and the way she clutched at me. That part knew that Holly wouldn't handle it well if I suggested the hospital.

"Do you want to tell me about it?" I asked, tentatively. I'd never had to ask my last miracle target anything. He'd been in his seventies, living alone, and just blurted everything out. Holly was different. She spent more time looking at her phone than me. It made it twice as hard to understand what was going on in her head. I knew she was hurt over Maddie's death. But she never talked about it.

My question just set off another round of crying. I guess it was the wrong thing to ask.

My back ached and my dress was soaked with tears by the time her crying subsided. Whatever was going on inside her was a battle; a different kind of battle than those I'd fought before. It was a bit unnerving. I couldn't see the bad guys. But it was also … very profound. Because eventually, Holly told me what was going on. Apparently, she didn't hate me. Or trash. She hated her parents.

"They cleared out Maddie's room and didn't even ask me!

Didn't tell me. My mom just said it was too hard to keep looking at everything. Close the fucking door, bitch! They got rid of everything. Donated it all. Then my boyfriend, Joe, called me whiny. So I broke up with him. And now he's unfollowed me on Insta," Holly started coughing from her tears. I patted her back for a second, but the coughing didn't stop, so I got up and got her a glass of water and brought over the Kleenex box, which ended up half empty before she was done blowing her nose and wiping her tears.

I tried to imagine what it would be like if I lost my brother, John. Angels were immortal. Unless of course, they warred with demons. John had been hurt once in a war. I'd flown to be by his side. I'd been afraid. Very afraid. But I didn't know what came after that fear, because I hadn't lost John. He'd been fine. I was at a loss.

"I'm so wasted," Holly moaned as she downed the glass of water, spilling half of it on herself. I grabbed a towel and helped her mop up. Physical messes I could deal with. But this?

"It looks like she never even existed," Holly sniffled; her throat raw and sore as her head rested on my shoulder. "They erased Maddie."

"People aren't pencils," I said as I stroked her blonde hair. "You can't erase them." I nearly brought up the "s" word but the manual was very clear. Establish trust first before talking about souls or the afterlife. Otherwise, I'd end up coming across as a prophet. People didn't tend to believe prophets so … I shut my mouth, hoping that Holly was starting to trust me. If trust was measured in tears, then she was. But again, the manual was vague on trust and what it meant to humans. Angels just trust God. We have no choice. But humans …

Holly gave a little snot-infused laugh. "Not literally erased. Sometimes you say the dumbest shit. But from our house, they did erase her. They took everything of hers away. They're the *worst* parents alive. I can't even—"

Ohh, now, *that* was in the manual. Finally! Something I could work with! I nearly did one of Amethyst's fist pump things. Apparently, according to roll number sixty-seven on the scroll, resenting parents was a teenage tradition that dated back centuries. It was best handled with something called 'commiseration.' Which meant I was to show her sorrow or pity. Yes! I could do that!

So, just like the heavenly manual instructed, I said, "I pity you."

Instead of making Holly smile and feel better, that made her sit up and look at me with a furrowed brow. She swiped at her nose as she studied me, her eyes curious under her long, fake lashes.

Was one expression of sympathy not enough? Did I need another? Cumulonimbus bunnies! Cutting off demon heads was so much easier. I sat back and stretched my sore back as I wracked my brain for something else to say. "I'm so sorry your parents seem unreasonable to you."

My words were met with dead silence. Was she thinking? Was my message sinking in? An excited little bubble of hope formed in the pit of my stomach. Sunrays! I hoped that I was having a breakthrough! Who needed a mentor anyway—

Holly stood up, fixing her clothes after being on the floor so long. She yanked at her oversized, off-the-shoulder green sweater as she stared down at me. "What the fuck, Ruby? I thought you were on my side! This is bullshit. I quit!" She grabbed her handbag.

Panic burbled in my stomach. It felt just like one of those moments before I took an arrow to the gut—I stood quickly, blood rushing to my head. "No! Wait! What?"

But, just like this afternoon, Holly didn't wait. She stomped off, around the mess she'd made, giving the stack of boxes one last kick for good measure.

"Holly—"

She was gone.

I sank onto my furry white rug and spread my wings as I stared up at the ceiling. I dimmed the light from heaven that lit my display cubbies. The loading dock door slammed shut behind Holly. Oh, hail. I covered my eyes with my hands and took a deep breath. But fear buzzed beneath my skin. I was failing again. Failing. Possibly even worse than last year. And I didn't even know why.

My eyesight smeared. And I realized I was crying again, just like earlier when I'd met the beautiful man with the broken shirt. His face flitted through my mind. He'd had warm brown eyes, and a dimple in his chin that was technically a manufacturing error, but still endearing. I hadn't learned his name. And now I regretted not asking him to come in and help. Tears dripped down my cheeks. And I let them, as I stared up at the blurry ceiling. "Help," I whispered. "Please God, help guide me."

Gunther's annoying light popped up right above my nose, nearly blinding me. "Help will be here tomorrow. Now get some sleep. And for goodness' sake, pick up in here before he arrives."

His light popped out of existence before I could respond. I just rolled over, swiped at my eyes, and fell asleep, hoping everything would be better in the morning.

It wasn't. It was the same.

Unlike in heaven, where the sunlight magically dusted the clouds with gold and clean robes appeared, pressed and warm and ready for us each morning, Earth did not have such logically functional amenities. Here, last night's disaster just looked worse in the morning light. The boxes Holly knocked over in her fit were everywhere. Mismatched shoes were scattered all over my floor. I knew my backroom was going to look the same. She toppled at least one rack back there.

I sat up and rubbed my eyes. Cleaning. A mentor. A rogue miracle target. "My day couldn't possibly get any worse."

Amethyst banged on the front door of my store and then

peered in the window at me, where I sat on my rug. My best friend was wearing a big fluffy black coat—it must be cold outside—and carrying an orange purse the size of a suitcase.

"Open up!" she yelled. For a little skinny person, she had quite the voice. My old choir master would have loved her. I liked her pretty well myself. Ever since she'd shown up in Silver Springs a month ago, we'd become fast friends.

"Come on! Lemme in! I have a surprise for you!"

I stretched and made my way to the door. I unlocked it and let her in, saying, "I hope it's a pumpkin spice latte … I love those things!"

"We can definitely grab one of those. But girl—shower first. You smell." She wrinkled her nose as she looked at me.

I sighed and led her up the stairs to my cramped living quarters over the shoe store. It was a tiny apartment, hardly more than a box, but it was painted white and clean. I could stretch my wings inside and that was all I really needed. Though my bed was hard and the furry rug downstairs was much softer. I told Amethyst everything that had happened with Holly.

Amethyst just shook her head and bit her lip. "Lady, geez. I can't believe you said that!"

"What do you mean? I was trying to show sympathy." Was our manual wrong? Was I supposed to show aggression?

Ugh! I hated—this word was seriously the best, how had no one said it to me before?—*Harmony's Guide*.

"Yeah," Amethyst snorted. "Well, you definitely didn't do that. What you said was sarcastic, not sympathetic." She ran a hand through her hair and sat down at my tiny, two-seater kitchen table. She dumped her purse out on the table and started sorting through the contents.

I took a quick shower, dried my hair with heaven's warm glow, and got dressed in a pink dress with a few decorative buttons down the front. I tried out a bit of lipstick, since Holly and Amethyst always went on about the stuff. My lips ended up a deep red, which I thought looked a bit ridiculous, like I'd smeared strawberry jam on my mouth, but apparently, looking like you were a sloppy eater was attractive to humans. I slipped on some white velvet starling shoes that rode the line between slipper and flat. I nearly moaned at their softness. These were the best shoes I'd found on earth yet. I blew them a little kiss before I grabbed my purse and wandered back toward Amethyst.

She was looking through my cabinets when I walked into my tiny, white fifties-style kitchen.

"I don't have food right now or I'd offer you some. I've got to go to the bank again and get more money."

Amethyst did her eye roll thing as she held up a pack of matches she'd found in a kitchen drawer.

I pointed at her. "Why did you roll your eyes? What did I

do that was annoying?" I took a step forward, concerned. How was going to the bank annoying? Or was she upset that I didn't have food? People did get mad about food. Holly showed me a Hangry commercial on her phone once. So, that *was* a thing. Even I didn't like being hungry. And I didn't technically have to eat more than every few days.

Amethyst grabbed a slip of paper from her purse. "You need to start selling shoes, Rub. You can't just keep letting that poor bank manager give you money."

"But banks are where people go to get money," I said.

"People get money that they intend to pay back," she corrected. "It's called a loan."

I started, gripping the back of a wooden chair. My wings flared just a little in surprise. "What!? I have to pay it back?"

Amethyst brushed her hand over her brow. Was that the thinking pose? I tried to recall the guide illustration. People always seemed to do that around me. "Rub, sometimes I wish you'd spent more time in the real world this last year and less time in the graveyard. Then you'd know how things work. I know you're trying honey, but you're just ... I'm trying to find a nice way to say this. You're out of touch. You have no common sense. None."

I sat down in the kitchen chair, disheartened. "Is that why Holly doesn't like me? Because of common sense?"

45

"Pretty much. But I might have a solution. Do you trust me?"

"Of course!" Amethyst was even better than Maddie when it came to teaching me about earth and people. Despite what her family thought, she was a really good person. She might be a curse-worker, but really it wasn't like she had a choice. She was born that way.

"Okay, great." Amethyst took a little slip of paper and lighter from her pile of purse stuff. She lit the paper on fire and held it in one hand. As it turned to ash, she put her other hand underneath to catch the ashes. She let the paper burn right down to her fingertips. Then she took the ashes and smeared them on my arms, chanting in Latin.

"Hoc animus est, et custodiunt."

I blinked and looked up at her. "Um, what are you doing?"

She didn't answer, just finished her chant. My arms started to glow purple. And then suddenly the ashes were absorbed by my skin. "What the *twinkly stars* have you done?"

Amethyst bit her lip. "I hope that glow goes away. I didn't think about that." She reached forward to stroke my arm but I yanked it back.

"Did you just curse me?"

She wavered her hand in front of her. Shock and fear rolled through me like fog because I knew that gesture from the handbook. It meant kinda. "Are you serious right now? You said we were BEF."

Amethyst tucked a strand of blonde hair behind her ears as she smiled apologetically. "It's BFF. And we are. I'm trying to help you."

My face heated up. It felt like everything from my neck up was on fire. I was so angry. I'd felt a lot of things since I'd come to this planet and been given an earthly body. Embarrassment, sadness, loneliness. But anger was a first for me. Angels were typically gifted with extreme calm. We needed to keep a clear head to complete our missions. Anger wasn't a heavenly emotion. It didn't come from the good place. It was a billowing inferno with lots and lots of smoke. Right now, my head was anything but angelically clear. My brain boiled. Part of me wanted to boil Amethyst. Preferably alive. *All the stars in heaven—did I really just think that? What's wrong with me? Oh goodness. Am I falling? Did she curse me to become a fallen angel?*

I took a menacing step toward the witch. But the balance thing got to me. And I tumbled face first to the floor. The smack was so hard I felt it in my bones.

Amethyst rushed over to me and helped pull me up. "Are you okay? That looked like a bad one."

I rubbed my nose, which still smarted something fierce, distracting me from my fury. Amethyst handed over some ice wrapped in a towel and I slapped it onto my aching nose. Ohhh. Ouch. The Mortal Bodies Comission was getting a complaint letter. Why would they make something on the face stick out when falling was such an issue on this planet? *Stupid gravity.*

I started.

I just cursed in my head. I said a bad word. I've never said a bad word. Holy shit—there's another!

"Rub—" Amethyst patted my back.

I turned to glare at her. It was her fault I was angry, her fault I'd fallen down, her fault I'd just said curse words—I took a deep breath. I had to get a handle on this anger. I closed my eyes and tried some deep breaths, letting the air whoosh in and out of my lungs and calm me. It seemed to work. The anger dimmed from a boil to a simmer, enough for me to open my eyes and look at her. "What did you do to me?"

"You're having a lot of trouble understanding humans. I thought you could use a little bit of humanity…" Amethyst trailed off in a way that let me know she didn't want to tell me exactly what she had done.

My stomach sank as I grabbed her hand. "Just say it."

"I gave you a little bit of a soul."

I reeled back, just like I had that one time a spearhead had pierced my armor. I felt like Amethyst had dropped me into a molten pit of lava. I plopped down right on the hardwood floor. For once I didn't even notice how uncomfortable it was. A soul? I had a human soul inside me? I stared down at my arms, ran my hands over the tiny hairs there. They stood up and I got goosebumps.

Only demons took in people's souls.

A pop sounded and Amethyst and I both reeled back.

Gunther's blazing giant ball of light took up half the room, blinding both of us. "Ruby!!! What have you done?"

"Me! I didn't do anything!!!" I protested.

"You let a dark witch put a curse on you! You took in part of a human soul! That's a strike!"

Panic popped in my stomach, like a whole sheet of that bubble wrap stuff compressing at once. This was bad. So bad. Two strikes. My breath started to come out in jagged gasps. *I am a two-strike angel. No. No.* My lips trembled. "But—"

His ball of light grew into an angry white mass that was so bright I had to close my eyes. Even then, the light pierced my eyelids with an awful bright yellow-green color.

"Wait! Can't you help me just get it out?" I pleaded. "Just take the soul away!"

"We don't do that! Taking souls from living beings is what *they* do!"

Gunther growled. "Get that miracle right, missy. Or you're looking at your final strike!"

My knees started to shake. And I nodded furiously, until it

felt like I was one of those spastic bobble-head dolls people stuck on their windshields. *Get it right. Get this miracle right.*

"Yes sir," I whispered.

Gunther disappeared with a loud bang that rang deep inside my eardrums.

Once he was gone, I turned to Amethyst, who was blinking hard and popping her jaw after Gunther's exit. "Girl, I promise, I'll help you get through this miracle. We'll fix this."

Fear and hope intertwined inside my chest. They wrestled with one another, neither able to win. They just ended up a confusing tangle of feelings. I put my hand over my heart. "Promise?"

She nodded. "But, if I'm gonna solve any celestial problems, I'm gonna need the nectar of the gods first."

I scrunched my brow. "Lots of people have used that saying. God doesn't drink nectar though. He likes water."

Amethyst rolled her eyes. "I meant coffee. Let's go get coffee."

She looped her arm through mine, and we went downstairs. I pulled in my wings so other supes couldn't see them; it was not very polite for me to stand in line and tickle everyone around me I'd learned. We strode past my disastrous showroom, and out onto the sidewalk.

"Are you sure coffee is gonna help you solve my problem?" I asked doubtfully. "I don't see how a drink can do that."

Amethyst winked at me. "Then you don't know enough about coffee. That stuff's pure magic."

She was right. Just not the way she expected.

CHAPTER 4

PARKER

"Let the pick-up line contest commence," I said as I checked my reflection in the living room mirror. I made sure the black horns on my forehead were invisible to supes, sometimes those pesky things liked to pop up at inconvenient times. They made it hard to convince the supernatural population to trust our repair shop after I fried their electronics. I waved a hand in front of them, adding a little extra magic to disguise my true form. I pushed back my long brown hair. I constantly debated trimming it, but something happened when I smiled at a woman and nervously pushed back my bangs after I'd zapped her phone. She'd give a little giggle. And that's how I knew I'd won. So, I kept my hair in a 90's falling-over-my eyes style. This human body I'd gotten was top-of-the-line. I knew a guy in Possessions. He'd traded for a full soul and gotten me this top-notch model, complete with abs and some pretty rocking biceps. The human who'd had this body before me had apparently been pretty vain. Model wannabe or something who'd traded his soul for an underwear gig. Only he'd been dumb enough to trade away the whole thing, leaving this awesome body ripe for the possessing. A few convos later and the pink slip was mine. As much as Migs might chip at me for my loquacious nature, chatting people up was how I'd managed to exist so long and get where I was. It got me favors. It helped me rise so that I was comfortably invisible in the middle of the pack. Nearly forgotten in the demon world. Nearly free.

I turned to Migs and Barrister as I sat down on a stool in the kitchen at our apartment, just above our shop. I leaned back on the white tile countertop. I had to shove aside one of Migs latest projects. The workaholic in him meant every room in our place was littered with some kind of computer gadget.

Bar smiled back at me and rubbed his hands together. "Hope you have cash on you. Because you're definitely doing the coffee run this morning. You're going down."

I smiled smugly, I had today's nerdiest pick up line competition in the bag. I'd been up trolling the internet last night while I worked on crashing those servers down in New York City. After Bar and I had come up with a plan to get Migs good and distracted so we could hunt down that witch today and get back part of his soul, I hadn't been able to sleep. I had found at least two zingers.

Migs rolled his eyes and yawned. He went first, like he always did. The practical one, he wasn't as competitive as Bar and me about bragging rights. When he won, he didn't even put his line on the whiteboard in the back-room of the shop. Bar and I never missed the chance to remind one another that we'd won. Migs shoved his hair back and adjusted his red plaid shirtsleeves, rolling them up and wiggling his fingers as he grinned. "Do you have eleven protons? Because you're sodium fine!"

Dammit! That was one of the ones I'd screenshotted. Shit. That'd teach me to look up pick-up lines instead of making up my own like Bar typically did.

I turned to my other competitor. Bar lounged against the wooden dining table, twirling a penlight between his fingers as he waited his turn. When he saw me look at him, he gave a naughty wink, the kind that had drawn me to him in the first place. Bar walked more on the edge of light and dark than Migs. He occasionally dipped his toe into the naughty pool. But overall, he was still a good person. Part of me wanted to change that. Part of me wanted to pull him down and keep him with me forever. But humans didn't fare as well in hell as demons. And so, the better part of me, the piece that housed a bit of his soul, didn't want that fate for him.

"Dude—what the fuck? Do I have egg in my teeth or something? Why are you staring?" Bar reached up and ran a finger over his teeth.

"You're just too damn pretty." I winked.

55

Migs chuckled as Bar chucked the penlight at me. I caught it.

"If that was your line, it sucked," Bar said.

"It wasn't. It's your turn. But you better hurry before I get a hard on from staring at you."

Both guys groaned. They weren't as sexually fluid as I was, though from the outside, their close friendship often made people wonder.

Bar grinned as he said, "Baby, I wanna play master/slave with *all* your devices."

FUCK NO! He'd stolen my second line. How the fuck— "Cheaters!" I grabbed my phone from my pocket and chucked it at Migs. I had no doubt he was the one who'd hacked it. Bar and I had been up late, and the dude had crashed hard when we got home, I'd heard him snoring.

Migs and Bar both chuckled as I punched each of them in the arm. "Fuckers."

Migs grinned, proud of himself. I rolled my eyes. The demon in me was proud of him, too. Shithead.

Migs glanced around me at the clock. "You have sixty seconds to come up with a winning pickup line. Or an equivalent to Bar's."

My heart started to pound fast. Even though this was a nothing contest, I loved a challenge. I wracked my brain. Of course, since we worked with phones and computers all day, those were the things that came to mind. "Are you a speed charger? Because right now, you've got my *device* 100% charged."

Migs grinned. "Decent. Lightning round—face off. Thirty seconds each. First to flop grabs coffee."

He turned to Bar, the baby-faced one in our group. Bar just smirked at me. "Wrote out five of my own yesterday, fucker. Prepare to go down." He pulled out a sheet of paper and cleared his throat. "Call me Google. Cause I'm gonna let you search my engine and then I'm gonna crawl *all over* you."

Dammit. Double whammy. I felt my blood pulse in my ears. The testosterone started racing. The need to win became a visceral thing and my damn horns popped back out. Migs couldn't see them, because he didn't know about the supernatural world, but Bar looked at me funny. I ignored him as I wracked my brain for computer knowledge. I'd been assigned to earth for thirty years, so I pulled out the old guns. "I'm gonna take it as slow as dial up so you'll scream like an old school modem."

Bar's hand fisted on his paper.

That's right, motherfucker! Demon's got game! I wobbled my head at him and made a stupid face to piss him off more.

He narrowed his eyes and glanced back at his list. "I bet I can guess your password. Is it "three orgasms?" If it isn't, I can help you change that."

"Can I connect to your *hotspot*?" I got breathy on the last word and leaned into Bar, batting my eyes until Migs was doubled over in laughter.

Bar slid down to the other side of the dining table. He cleared his throat and blinked his pretty brown eyes. He bit his lip with an innocent expression. "My head's always in the cloud. But now that I've seen you, my heart's there, too."

Everyone froze. *What the motherfuck? Sweet? He'd pulled out sweet? Dammit all to fucking hell.*

"Winner!" Migs declared, pointing at Barrister.

Black claws popped out in place of my fingernails and my teeth elongated to fangs.

Bar didn't even blink an eye. He'd seen me go full demon before. "You like that bitch? I got more where those came from." Then he turned around and started twerking as he rapped, "Girl, call me GoDaddy when you back that app up. Back that app up."

Migs and I collapsed in laughter as Barrister turned around and said, "That's right. Don't mess with the master."

Migs shook his head, gasping even as he pointed. "That last one is so inaccurate. I can't even. GoDaddy doesn't host apps."

Bar shrugged. "It still rocked."

I sighed and dug into my pockets for my wallet. I checked for cash. I never used a card because of the electronic trail it left, since, technically, my human was dead. "Guess I'm taking orders. What do you idiots want to drink?"

I rolled my eyes as I walked into Jewels Cafe, joining the line there. I inhaled the fresh scent of coffee and smiled. I waved my hand and fried two phones, as the people behind me walked in with their heads glued to their screens. One guy started complaining right away. The other just stared at his phone in disbelief. I turned my head to avoid that bunny shifter that worked here; he was in the corner, his brown hair had this close crop on the sides to make him look more badass. It really just made him easier to pick out in a crowd. Which was good for me, because he immediately sat up in his chair by the window and eyed the two guys with messed up phones as they complained. I knew that bunny shifter was into some kind of social media or something and I'd fried his laptop often enough that he was suspicious of me.

I turned toward the opposite side of the cafe and gave him my back as I double checked that my horns weren't showing in the window reflection. I had to tweak the magic a little because one of them popped out. I slid forward and a tall guy blocked the bunny shifter from view. I studied the menu. It wasn't until I'd finished deciding on my order and took a step forward when the line moved that I noticed her. Once I did, I couldn't believe I'd been able to look at anything else.

The woman in front of me had gorgeous, flowing hair that fell in waves down her spine. Her ass was a perfect bubble beneath a pink skirt that highlighted its perfection.

ANN DENTON

Her voice drifted back over to me and was as melodic as a harp. Everything about her called to me. I even had a stupid thought that I liked her shoes. They were flats that showed she was practical and not all hung up on appearances. I bumped into her "accidentally," hoping she'd turn around. She did.

And fire and brimstone. She was so hot she was volcanic. She had straight brows, deep grey eyes, and this large bottom lip I couldn't stop staring at. Not to mention her hourglass figure. Fuck. "Sorry, I'm clumsy," I muttered.

Instead of rolling her eyes like I expected, her face brightened at that. "Oh, I am too! I think it's the boobs for me though, always messing up my balance."

Her friend—a blonde woman—face palmed next to her. "Ruby, we don't talk about boobs to strangers."

I held out my hand, "Hi, I'm Parker. See, not a stranger. Feel free to talk to me about boobs all you want."

Ruby grinned and took my hand. Her head tilted and she wore a puzzled expression. "Have we met before?"

"I'm pretty sure I would have remembered you," I said, stroking the back of her hand with my thumb. "It's not often I meet angels in real life."

She stiffened and then twisted, her hand still in my grip. "Are my wings showing? Shoot! I thought I did that spell to retract them right."

My heart froze. My system errored. My entire existence

went 404—page not found. No. No. No. No. I scanned the coffee shop, which was buzzing with humans and supernaturals alike. Was there a torture demon in here? Some upper management devil from a lower ring of hell sent just to smack me down? They generally focused on humans but ... I studied every face in the coffee shop. There was the blonde barista, her bear mate sweeping the floor. Human. Human. I didn't see another of my kind, even in disguise. I would have been able to sense them. Then what the fuck? Why was I drawn to an angel? A god-loving enemy?

I turned back to Ruby and my words came out scratchy. "You're really an angel?"

She blinked. "Oh, wait. I thought you were a supernatural. I saw a horn flicker and just thought billy-goat shifter. Are you not a supe?" Her hand smacked her cheek. "I'm not supposed to tell non-supes. Darn it."

My ego didn't even have time to be bruised by the billy-goat thing. The little shred of Bar's soul inside me was too busy clawing at itself, flagellating its back, crying and bemoaning our fate. I agreed, so wrapped up in self-pity that I didn't notice when Ruby extracted her hand from mine and went to place her order. I forgot to move forward until the guy in line behind me tapped me on the shoulder.

I put in an order; I didn't even know if it was the right one. I felt dazed, kind of like I had centuries ago when I'd been stationed on a planet helping out with a Great Cleansing. We'd won, the bad guys had taken the planet.

But I'd felt awful about it. I was an awful warrior demon. Killing had never been my strong suit. I was much more comfortable in the annoyance and bad mood realm of hell. That was where I thrived. Ticking people off. Instigating political conversations that led to shouting matches and ended friendships. That was more fulfilling to me than dead bodies. Because dead was done. Over. And half the people we killed were possibly going to heaven anyway. But having someone stub their toe, then lose their keys, drop their phone in the toilet? Those torturous possibilities were endless. They could go on for years.

I didn't know of anyone ever torturing a demon and an angel via attraction. Humans, sure, all the time. Making them think that someone was their soulmate when they were actually a match made in hell—there was a whole division for that.

Oh shit. Soul. Soulmate. I had part of a human soul. Did angels have souls? I hadn't looked at the Angelic Cheat Codes for centuries.

If angels had souls … was Ruby … Barrister's soulmate?

I felt like that witch in that movie that got crushed by a house. Everything but my feet felt smashed flat. I fucking hated Bar for a second, jealousy lighting up every nerve ending in my body.

I glanced over at Ruby, who had slid into a seat and was blowing the steam off her coffee mug. Her wings flickered into view for a second, before she waved her hand and made them invisible again. But even just that glimpse had me wanting to stroke them, to see if they were as soft as they looked. My heart pulsed so hard I felt it in my throat. Everything in that little scrap of soul I had was drawn to her, wanted her, needed her.

Fuck.

She took a sip of her drink. And then her eyes rose to meet mine.

It felt like I'd been tossed into the middle rung of hell. Like I was melting in lava. I was pure molten need. I burned for her. Every part of my body ached because I wasn't touching her. Because we were apart. My vision grew tunneled. I didn't see anything else. Just her. I took a step toward her and she stood, taking a half step toward me, her arm stretching out, fingers reaching for me. Mine mirrored it, like some goddamned disgusting slow-motion Hallmark scene. Or that damned ceiling that dead dude painted. But even as I mocked myself, I couldn't stop it. I had to touch her. Had to.

Her friend stood at the table, chair scraping backward as she latched onto Ruby's arm and pulled my woman off balance.

My woman.

I rushed forward to pull Ruby back from her. But the blonde woman stepped between us. Her eyes flickered back and forth between me and Ruby as we held eye contact and sought out one another's hands around her.

The blonde smacked our hands down. "Outside," she commanded and jerked her head toward the door of the coffee shop.

I offered my elbow like some weird old-fashioned idiot. But Ruby took it. When she touched me, my entire body hummed. Yes. This was right. So goddamned fucking right.

I led Ruby through the throng of people and out onto the cobblestone sidewalk. Her friend marched ahead, giving death glares at everyone walking by until she'd cleared a space for us. Then she whirled around.

"Amethyst," Ruby asked, as her fingers stroked the crook of my elbow. "What is it?"

Amethyst pointed an accusing finger at me. "This demon's trying to get you axed. He just put a mating spell on you!"

CHAPTER 5

RUBY

"Demon!" I turned to stare up at Parker's handsome face, which was drawn and serious. His horns were visible again. Two little black bumps. But those weren't demon horns. Demon horns were long and curled and—dammit all to hell (oh shit, I cursed again!) I was thinking of warrior demons. Those were what I knew. Vicious, black, scaled demons who swung swords and tried to remove my head from my body. But, obviously, there were other types of demons. Was Parker some other kind of demon?

"I didn't put a spell on you," Parker whispered.

"The fuck you didn't!" Amethyst snapped. "I can see the spell connecting you two. It's a bright red, fiery rope."

Parker grabbed my hand from his elbow and held it gently

65

between his. His hands felt good, warm and strong and slightly rough. "I wouldn't do that to you, Ruby. I promise. I saw you and I just, immediately, was drawn to you."

I swallowed hard, torn between lust and pure terror. My human body vibrated, practically singing with emotions. My eyes teared up for some reason, which made Parker give me a tortured look, which in turn only added to the vicious internal whiplash I was experiencing.

My cheeks burned. My throat closed. My fingers tingled under Parker's touch. My nipples tightened and my feet shuffled closer to him, studying his brown eyes beneath the rectangle-frame glasses he wore. I reached up with my free hand and adjusted his crooked, dull-gold bow tie.

Somehow, that gesture felt intimate. And right. It made his breath catch.

I watched him swallow hard and I found myself doing the same as a hot, tingling sensation shot through my human body and settled near my loins.

"Fuck," I whispered.

"Yes. Let's," he whispered back.

Amethyst wedged herself bodily between us. "No. Let's not. You're going through some sort of magical weirdness right now. Who knows? Maybe it was that bit of soul I put into you—maybe that dude I got it from was a demon sex fiend—"

"Soul?" Parker asked, turning back to look at me.

I blushed hard and my wings popped out, my magic shield failing in my embarrassment. "She gave me a little bit of human soul to help me with common sense."

Parker stumbled back a step. His eyes narrowed at Amethyst. "Wait. What was your name?"

My BEF crossed her arms. "None of your beeswax."

I had no idea what bees had to do with this conversation, but I sensed this wasn't the time to ask.

Parker looked back over at me. "Is this *Amethyst?*"

I nodded.

His face paled. He dropped his travel tray full of coffees at our feet and we all had to jump back in order to avoid the scalding liquid. But that meant that I lost my balance—of course. My arms windmilled and Parker leapt forward to save me from face-planting in the hot brown puddle of coffee.

His arms wrapped around me and he lifted me up. His touch made my head into a hazy, cloudy mess full of rain-drops and rainbows. His hand slid past my butt and my brain lit up a bright blazing red that made me want to rub against him like I'd seen cats do to trees or women do to men in music videos, though why men stood like trees and let women spread their scent on them like cats was just plain confusing.

I opened my mouth, about to ask Parker about this cat-like urge, but then he swung me around so that he carried me bridal style, surprising me. He leaned down and his forehead nearly touched mine, energy crackling between us as he said, "I need you to come home with me. There's someone you need to meet."

He ran before Amethyst could stop him, pulling me tight against him. He was so fast that everything blurred around us. I could hear her shouting a hex as he rounded the corner, but her purple blast of magic shot down the street and hit a tree instead. Its leaves shriveled.

I tried to protest, but Parker's arms felt so good and suddenly I couldn't remember English. I could only think in Aramaic, in Gloobish, in Kirackadoo. But all those thoughts amounted to the same thing: If this was what kidnapping looked like, if this was the dark side, sign me the fuck up!

Amethyst chased after us, screaming. People in the streets turned to stare at her. I watched her over Parker's shoulder—she was such a good friend to try and defend me against the enemy. Just like a soldier! Only, Parker wasn't the enemy. I looked up at him. Was he? He didn't feel like the enemy. I could feel his heart pounding against my side as he ran up a hill. His breath was minty, and his clothes had a soft Downy-fresh scent. He didn't smell like the enemy. Demons smelled like fire and brimstone.

Maybe Amethyst was confused. Maybe she'd had a spell put on her? She was a curse-worker. It seemed more likely that she'd be a curse target than me. *That seems right,* I thought, as I snuggled into Parker's arms, admiring his bicep and trying to resist that annoying cat-like urge to rub my face against it. *Poor Amethyst had a curse that made her see a goat shifter as a demon. I felt bad for her. Maybe she needs a miracle from me, too.*

I glanced back. Amethyst had run out of breath and bent in half, her hands grabbing onto her knees as she struggled to take in air. Parker didn't even seem winded. Of course, his body was full of muscle that rubbed deliciously against me, sending those hot tingles through me every so often, particularly when his fingers clenched down on my hips.

My hand twitched, interested in reaching up and tracing the square line of his jaw.

I had to hold myself back. I had to remind myself that Amethyst said he was a demon. That this was a major problem, even if she was delusional. I had to remind myself that I was a two-strike angel. He might not feel like the enemy, but I was having human emotions. And human emotions were insane. And I couldn't afford any other mistakes. *In fact—shit!—I should be back home cleaning up, getting ready for my mentor!*

I wriggled out of Parker's hold when he came to a stop. "I —we—" my English failed me, and I just ended up shaking my head.

Parker pressed his lips together. "I know. I know. I just need you to meet someone—"

His words were interrupted when the door behind him

swung open. The door to what looked like a computer shop, if the display window was anything to go by.

"Hey, dickhead, where's our coffee?" A hot guy with dark hair joked as he leaned against the door, partially blocked from view by Parker's broad shoulder.

Something about the guy's voice seemed familiar. I leaned around Parker to look at the other man. To my surprise, I recognized him. He was wearing a shirt today. But he was the man who'd stood by me last night when I'd cried. The man who'd offered to help me.

My throat tightened as I remembered just how sweet he'd been. I hadn't noticed in the shadows, with his baseball cap on and everything, but he was handsome. His black hair gleamed in the morning light and his thick brows were the broody kind that Amethyst loved in that *Xena* show she'd had me watch. He had Ares-level brows. And his warm, coffee-colored eyes met mine.

It was the moment in the coffee shop all over again.

Zing. Bang. Boom. All those cartoon explosion words. My chest ached like a hole had been blown inside it, a hole only he could fill.

The guy's jaw fell open.

That meant scared, right? *Shit!* I looked behind me to make sure no demons were gathering, that Parker hadn't led me into a trap, or Amethyst hadn't magically caught up and hurled a hex our way. But no one was there. I turned back to the two men. My heart thrummed hard as Parker went to stand beside the other guy.

My heart tugged at me. It demanded I get closer to both of them. I was too far away. A space low in my stomach heated and throbbed. My entire body rebelled against my mind, which wanted to know what the hell was going on. Was this what humanity was like? No wonder Holly was crazy.

My feet strode toward Parker and the man with the sweet soul that I'd met last night. Even in the crisp light of morning, I could see the bright edges of his soul high-lighting his skin. His soul was a light orange color. I noticed Parker had a flicker of the same color near his heart.

Parker gestured toward me and clenched his fist before he shoved his hand into his pocket. "Barrister, meet Ruby. I think … well, I can't be sure without Migs but—I think she's …" His face contorted like he was having trouble saying the words. "I think she's got what you've been looking for," he finished.

Barrister didn't say anything. He just stared at me, eyes drinking me in as I took in the sight of him. He was over six feet tall and I knew he had abs as hard as boulders underneath his shirt. I'd seen him look sweet, concerned, what I think might have been embarrassed, but now he just stared in a way I couldn't even begin to interpret. It was intense.

"What are you thinking?" I whispered. For some reason, I felt nervous about his answer. Was he judging me? Is that what his look meant? Was he rejecting me? A nervous shudder ran through me and I felt like I should jump on top of him and attack him with kisses so that he couldn't get the words 'go away' out. I resisted, but mostly because I was pretty sure if I tried to leap on him, I'd face plant into the door instead.

"Is this real?" Barrister finally asked. "Or is this some kind of joke?" He turned to Parker. "I swear dude, if you've pulled something on her, I will rip you a new one."

Parker shook his head. "No joke. Do you feel it? The connection?"

Bar nodded.

I took a step forward. "What is it? This connection?"

Parker's hand reached out and he gently tucked a strand of hair behind my ear. Barrister groaned at that and moved forward to run a finger over my other forearm. "You don't have to let him—us—touch you."

My body felt like it might combust. I felt swollen and full of a need for—*damn fucking English!*—I didn't even know what. But I pressed the back of Barrister's hand into me so that all of his fingers connected with my skin. His touch warmed me like sunshine.

"I think—you might be soulmates," Parker whispered, pushing up against me from the side.

Bar's hand closed around my arm and he pulled me into

him until my breasts pressed against his. "How's that possible?" he whispered. "You're an angel, right?"

My tongue failed me. I could only nod my head, awash in sensations. *Holy fuck! Why didn't every angel snag a bit of soul? This feeling, this light-heading feeling, was better than the rush I felt when I dove through the clouds and waited as long as I could to spread my wings. It was better than the soft fluffiness of clouds. It was better than anything*—as Parker and Barrister pressed against me, I felt connected to others in a way I'd never known was possible.

Angels always went on and on about humans and their torrid love affairs, as if love was something scandalous and awful. But how—why? This was amazing. This feeling was indescribable.

Barrister looked over at Parker. "How?" he asked again, reminding us of his question.

"Her friend said something about a soul. Ruby has a little piece of soul in her. I think it belongs to Migs—" Parker said softly.

"What the fuck, you two?" A new voice demanded from inside the building. "Where's my café?"

Parker wrapped an arm around me and pulled me inside the shop. Bar followed.

"Shut the door," Parker said. "And put the 'Closed' sign out."

"What?" the man inside asked.

My eyes adjusted to the dim interior light and a swoon-worthy guy walked toward me. He had blue eyes and brown hair swept back so his bangs somehow defied gravity. Stubble lined his upper lip and his jaw, giving his otherwise perfect features a gruff look. He was perfect. Except for the fact that he wore the one thing that Maddie had warned me all untrustworthy men wore. Plaid.

I stumbled back a step or two in horror, catching my foot on the rug.

Parker caught me before I could fall backward and crack open my skull.

He leaned down and said, "It's okay, Ruby. This is my roommate, Migs. I think you have a bit of his soul."

"What?" I pulled out of Parker's arms and ran to the other side of the room. "No! No!" I clutched at my hair, my breasts, my face in agony.

"What's she doing?" Migs asked, and even the sound of his voice was like a mooring, pulling me closer, reeling me in. My body struggled against my mind and I felt like trashing their place—just like Holly had trashed mine. *Fuck this!*

"I think she's freaking out about having your soul," Parker said.

"She's freaking out?" Barrister chipped in. "What about fucking me? I'm freaking out! Are you saying Migs and I are soulmates?"

"Yup," Parker responded.

"I'm not fucking soulmates with a fucking dude!"
Barrister yelled.

The guys started bickering in low tones, but I didn't listen.
I searched for an escape or a weapon, reverting to warrior
angel mode. This room was sadly lacking in either. There
were just little green squares and colored wires. It was
actually a giant mess. I had to make do with a mini screwdriver, which I turned and brandished. "You let me go or
I'll stab you all."

Barrister and the new guy Migs looked shocked—their
eyes wide.

Parker just laughed. "You're an angel. You can't stab
humans. You definitely can't stab your soulmate. And I've
got a bit of Bar's soul, so you can't stab me either—we are
technically soulmates, too. Good luck stabbing Migs.
Since you share a soul with him, I don't think your hand
will even let you get close."

I jabbed the screwdriver in his direction. "Don't mock me.
Amethyst was probably right. You probably are a demon."
I circled around them, back toward the entrance.

"I didn't say she wasn't."

"What?" My heart fell. She wasn't cursed? He was a
fucking demon? I nearly dropped the screwdriver, which
made me bend forward as I fumbled to get it—which
meant I was too top heavy with the damn boobs—and I
went plunging face first toward the floor. This time,

Parker wasn't close enough to save me. I hit the cement floor cheek first, which made my vision blur.

The man named Migs was closest and he hurried forward. He helped me sit up, and once my eyes cleared, I could feel two things clearly: a painful throbbing in my cheek and a strange dizzy sensation that hurtled through me as I looked at Migs. I felt completion, comfort, companionship—all kinds of words I'd come across when I'd studied human emotional needs. I felt whole for the first time in my existence.

I glanced down at his shirt. How could this be? How could I feel good when he touched me? "But—but, only assholes wear plaid."

Bar punched the air behind me. "Fuck yes! That's right, soulmate. Been telling the fucker that for years."

Migs just stared at me in concern. "Why did you call Parker a demon?" he asked.

My eyes traveled over to Parker and Migs, who were suddenly avoiding eye contact.

Ah shit. I'd just outed the paranormal world to a human.

CHAPTER 6

Migs

I sat back on my ass on the concrete floor, next to the hot-as-sin chick that had stumbled into our store. My mind was reeling. I blinked and tried to make sense of what was going on. The brunette in front of me—she was *the one*. I just knew it. Some stupid, primal ape-brain part of me knew she was *it*. I was pretty pissed at my brain right now because it had picked a woman who was clearly insane. She hated plaid, believed in demons, and had threatened me with a deadly weapon. I mean, the screwdriver was three inches long, but through the eye at the right angle and velocity? It'd kill me in two seconds flat.

Ruby adjusted her skirt, and my eyes were drawn to her pale thighs.

I snapped my gaze away; I didn't need the lust part of my

brain lighting up like a carnival ride. I focused on Bar and Parker instead, who were both staring at me with worried expressions. Parker had some kind of shit on his forehead, so I lifted my hand and pointed, "You got something—" I gestured, showing him that he'd gotten grease or something on his forehead.

He didn't wipe the marks away. Instead, he bent down and grabbed my hand, pulling me to my feet. "We need to talk."

I realized the marks on his forehead weren't just marks, they were horns.

"Dude, did Bar get you into cosplay now, too?" I asked, gesturing at Parker's mini horns. They looked a little like Daredevil's horns, small and pointed. "Or did you lose a bet?" I felt put out for a second that they were leaving me out of bets.

But Parker shook his head.

I frowned. Not cosplay and not a bet. A joke? I glared at Parker. Bar wouldn't pull shit on me. But I hadn't known Parker as long, just since we'd graduated college three years ago. Was this some kind of prank?

I asked, "Are you trying to get back at me for the pickup line thing? Chingón, Bar totally kicked your ass."

"Excuse me, what's a chinkun? Is that like a chicken?" Ruby asked. "I forgot to bring my dictionary."

"He's saying nasty things in Spanish," Bar corrected.

"Oh, a romance language! Those make so much more sense than English!"

I stopped short. I looked at her again, my eyes tracing the soft curves of her body and the sweep of her jaw. I got the urge to nibble her neck and whisper all kinds of naughty things in Spanish to her. "You don't like English?" I asked, studying her big grey eyes. I had to swallow hard when she shook her head.

"It's the worst! It's chaos! There are more words without rules than *with* them!"

"Yes!" I found myself stepping toward her. "I mean, I've been here eight years, but still. Yes!"

"And then, English doesn't stop at words that don't make sense. I have this teenage employee and she uses all these words wrong! When she says "chill" she doesn't mean cold, she means to spend time with someone. What? She just took a word and completely erased the original definition! How is anyone supposed to learn this language when people do things like that!" She stomped a foot.

"Yes!" I took another step toward her. Her annoyance at stupid English made my throat dry and my dick hard. No one else understood here. They all grew up in this disorganized chaotic mess of words. But she was the literal embodiment of my own frustration. "I know! How about when people just randomly cut off a word? Like fam. I cannot stand when people say that word. It's *family*. Don't be lazy. Your tongue can handle three syllables."

She took another step toward me, "Yes! Yes! I agree!"

"Why do we call it rush hour when the cars hardly move?" I asked.

"Why is it a toothbrush when you use it on more than one tooth?" Ruby's breath grew sultry.

Her thighs brushed against mine and her eyes burned with a passion I hadn't seen in a woman in years. I got lost in her eyes as, somehow, my hands made their way to her hips.

I murmured, "The word hit is completely overused. Hit on, hit the gas, hit it and quit it. Never the same meaning." My fingers flexed, digging into her soft curves.

She sucked in a deep breath, those big eyes of hers dilating as she stared up at me and asked, "Why are they called tennis shoes when you don't use them … for tennis?"

I felt her nipples pebbling against my stomach. Ruby smiled up at me and it took every ounce of self-restraint I had not to bend forward and ravage her lush mouth.

But then she said, "I've been on Earth a year and still— every day—I just feel so lost!"

"On Earth?" I took a step back. Shit. Right. She was delu-sional. A psychopath off her meds. I had to breathe deeply to calm my heart, which was screaming all sorts of nonsense at my head. Nonsense like, *she's telling the truth, I can tell.* Parker had probably paid her to say all that shit. My dick twitched in disagreement.

"I guess since I already told you about supes, it'd be okay if I showed you my wings." She waved a hand and a set of wings appeared on her back. Real fucking wings. With feathers and all.

I narrowed my eyes. I couldn't tell if she was joking or not. Her face looked serious, but was she being sarcastic? She had to be. This was nuts. But where did those wings come from? My lungs closed a bit as I backed up toward an aisle full of computer repair parts. Space. I needed space.

Bar called out, "It's not a joke, Migs. She's telling the truth. She's an angel. Ruby, can you fly?"

Her wings started to flutter, and I blinked in disbelief as her feet rose off the floor.

Impossible. That's fucking impossible. No. No way.

My grandmother Maria's voice sounded in my head, whispering in Spanish. She'd hated my skeptical nature, always lighting candles and praying for me when I was younger. "One day, mijo, you'll find your way back. I saw it in a dream." And now a woman was flying in midair in front of me. A woman who claimed she was an angel.

I shook my head, hand flying to my forehead to check for fever. My elbow knocked some graphics cards over, causing a domino effect down the shelf. But I didn't turn to look at them ... because suddenly, Ruby started to glow.

Her entire body was surrounded by a warm, golden light —the exact kind of light mi abuela Maria had said she'd experienced during her stroke. *Dios mio! Shit!*

Goosebumps rose up on my arms, and a cold fear trickled down my spine like ice. Was I about to be smited? Smote? Smitten? Fucking English!

A halo appeared over Ruby's head.

It felt like an out-of-body experience. I was witnessing the impossible. Or—what my abuela would have called—the possible, just not probable.

The glow faded as Ruby touched down near me. "So … hi," she waved shyly. "I'm Ruby and I'm an angel."

I doubted she knew she sounded just like an advertisement for a twelve-step program. But she did. My mouth quirked up a bit. Whatever vice Ruby was selling, I wanted it. She could have said she was a meth-head and I might not have cared. Because something in me was drawn to her like we were two halves of an orange. That inner voice whispered the Spanish version of that saying, "Sos mi media naranja." It was the phrase my grandfather used to say to my grandmother every morning when she handed him his café.

Ruby reached for my hand and when she touched me the truth of her words flipped a switch, like turning on a light bulb. If anyone else had said it—shit, Parker had tried to tell me two or three times he was a demon—I wouldn't have believed it. But I felt connected to her, knew I could trust her. And I couldn't explain why. Was it the soul thing? It had to be.

Souls were real.

Fuck.

I turned to Bar, even as I shifted Ruby's hand in mine so I could grip hers more tightly, squeezing her small fingers underneath mine. "What did you say about soulmates?"

Bar rolled his eyes. "I think Parker's jacked that bit up. We —" he gestured between us, "are *not* soulmates. Because that's bullshit! Unfair crap! But souls are real. That deal you made with the witch? Real. Luckily, she's Ruby's friend and gave your bit of soul to Ruby and not some shit monster."

I felt like an idiot, just like when I first moved to the U.S. and realized I knew nothing about this country, that everything I'd seen on television was a lie. Here I was again. On the precipice of a whole new world. I knew fuck-all about angels and demons and whatever else was out there. I hadn't thought souls were real. But glancing at Ruby, I knew they were.

I cleared my throat uncertainly. "Are shit monsters real?"

Bar laughed. "Who the fuck knows?"

Parker raised a hand. "Not only are they real, but you really don't want to get involved with them. It's messy."

"Was that a joke?" Bar wrinkled his nose.

Parker shook his head. "No. They literally trail shit everywhere. It's disgusting and unsanitary."

I shook my head. "This … is just hard to believe." I pulled Ruby closer and stroked the tip of her wing. The feathers were real. And so soft. Touching her made me feel more grounded, more secure, as I looked back over at Bar. "You. Fuckhead. You're supposed to be my best friend and you didn't tell me all this?"

Bar shook his head. "Dude, you're so … pragmatic. I tried to toss it out there a few times—"

I waved him off and turned to Parker. "Did you know we were soulmates this whole time?"

Bar interjected, "We're not soulmates!"

I ignored him, slightly irritated by his rejection.

Parker shrugged, leaning against the wall next to the door. "Why do you think I kept trying to get a threesome going?"

Ruby blinked and tugged on my hand. "What's a three-some?" she asked.

Just hearing that word come out of her mouth in that innocent tone—shit. Bar and Parker stepped forward, and I knew she'd had the same effect on them. Lust tinted the edges of my vision red and my dick tented in my pants. I had to take a tiny step away from her to remain a gentleman. But I didn't let her hand go.

"Oh, beautiful, it's so much easier to show you a threesome than explain," Parker was crowding me two seconds later, his hand caressing my Ruby's face.

I pushed him back. "Dude. Respect."

He pointed at his chest. "Demon. Temptation."

Bar shoved him aside and lifted Ruby's free hand to his lips. He placed a gentle kiss there. "Ruby, don't listen to these fools. As far as I'm concerned, you're a miracle—"

Ruby yanked her hands away from me and Bar. Her hands flew to her cheeks. "Miracles! Shit! Miracles! My mentor's about to get here—"

And she went running for the door. She had it unlocked and yanked open before I could stop her. She was booking it down the sidewalk when her ankle suddenly twisted. Her shoe went flying off and she fell with a huff to the sidewalk, her skirt flying up so I could see just a hint of lacy white panties.

Bar beat me to the door, running down the street and scooping Ruby up to coo over her. *Fuckwad.*

Parker went and scooped up the lost shoe. He slid it onto Ruby's foot as she sat suspended in Bar's arms. "Look, perfect fit. My princess." His hand traveled up her leg.

She winced and I yanked his hand away. "Don't hurt her!"

"I wasn't hurting her!" Parker argued.

Bar rolled his eyes.

Ruby interrupted what was sure to be a fight. "I'm so

sorry. I have to get back to my store and clean it up. I have a … mentor," she spat out that word like it was a fly that had flown into her mouth, "and he's going to arrive today."

Parker shook his head sympathetically. "Mentor? That's rough. I can give him a hard time if you want."

Ruby gave a little tinkling laugh that made me want to punch Parker in the chest. Instead, I yanked on his arm and pulled him toward the front door of our shop. I shoved him in front of me and muttered, "Find your keys. Mine are inside."

"Geez. What's your problem?"

I couldn't tell him that I fucking wanted to rip his arm off for touching Ruby when she was hurt—because that was goddamned insane. He wasn't trying to hurt her. But she was mine. Possessiveness threatened to make me blind with rage. I had to look away and recite my latest video game stats to make it recede. I ended up grunting, "Just do it."

Parker grumbled as he messed with his keys. "Woulda' thought seeing the light would make you nicer."

"Maybe I belong in hell," I shrugged. I had been a non-believer after all. Wasn't that where non-believers went?

Parker grinned as he locked up Computer and Phone Repair. He slung an arm around my shoulders. "Nah, man. If you belonged there, I'd have sent you off long ago."

The dark undertone, and the reality that he might, actually, possibly, be able to do that, sent a shiver down my spine.

Parker just laughed. "Dude, relax. I'm just a lowly tech demon. I fry electronic shit to piss people off and make them chip at each other. It's why Bar gave me a piece of that sugar a long time ago."

My entire world flipped for a second time in a single morning. "You mean that's how we've been getting customers!" *Cheating. With a demon.* I had to admit—it was fucking brilliant of Bar. *Asshole.*

Parker pointed up at Ruby, whose legs had parted a little as Bar held her, creating an inviting shadow underneath her skirt. I could almost see—or imagine I saw—those pretty lace panties again. The spot held me mesmerized.

Parker leaned over and whispered in my ear. "Now, do you want to talk about me, or do you want to help me figure out how to get our pure-as-light soulmate to agree to an orgy?"

Since logic was a falsehood and had no part in this world of angels and demons, I tossed it aside. Why use my brain when everything I'd ever thought was obviously a lie? I let my dick think for me.

And his thoughts were clear.

Corrupting my soulmate was his number one priority.

CHAPTER 7

RUBY

BARRISTER'S DEEP GAZE ALMOST MADE ME FORGET WHAT I was supposed to do. But the sun flashed through some trees behind him and the bright, obnoxious light reminded me of Gunther. "I have to get back to my shop," I said, my voice catching and going breathy.

He nodded. "I remember where it is. Do you think you can walk, or do you want me to carry you?"

Strange flutters started in my stomach. Was I going to be sick? Dammit! He was being so sweet! My stupid human body was ruining the moment. Dumb balance. His fingers grazed my back and a shiver went down my spine. Shivers? Yup. My body was definitely acting weird. And *Harmony's Guide* did state that puking was not used as a form of greeting on this planet. I wiggled down from

Bar's arms and said, "I think I can walk," though I really didn't want to. I wanted to snuggle against the hard planes of his chest a bit longer and put off this horrid mentor business altogether.

But angels don't get what they want. That's reality. What we want isn't important.

The fact that I wanted to find a way to make our skin liquid and melt into Barrister, Parker, and Migs (the way that Crocozoan aliens did when they mated) was unimportant.

My miracle was important.

Holly was important.

Humans were important.

Not angels.

"Stupid-ass rules," I muttered as I started limping toward my store.

"I agree," Parker glided up to take my arm and help me. "Rules are stupid. But what rule are we talking about exactly?"

"Where humans have it better than angels."

"Completely agree," Parker said as he tugged me closer so that my side brushed his as we walked. "Demons get the shaft too. It's why I've got a strict 'revel-in-obscurity' policy. I do just enough to not be noticed."

My eyebrows shot up and a giggle escaped me. "That's so

smart!" I'd only ever competed against my stupid brother, who seemed to excel at everything angelic. The only assignment I'd ever excelled at was the warrior angel bit because those rules were easy. "I wish I'd thought of it before I got two strikes."

Migs hurried up and snatched me away from Parker's side. He lifted me in his arms and wrapped my legs around his back. "I'm out of the loop here. Explain what that means."

I started to explain. I really did. But with my legs wrapped around Migs, my thighs and other areas rubbed against him and a strange warmth spread through my stomach. This body of mine was just out of control. Maybe it was broken. Because it was over-heating *down there*. "My tinder box is getting hot," I said, warning him.

Parker laughed. Bar blushed. But Migs looked confused.

"That was what they called it in the *Guide to Humans*," I said, struggling to remember the bit on human anatomy. "But they had a few different names for it. Because— English." I rolled my eyes. "Maybe you'll know one of the others. My lady's toupee? Petticoat lane? Mount Pleasant?" I cocked my head to see if any of the words registered.

Migs stopped dead. He swallowed a few times before whispering, "Are you saying ... your pussy is hot?"

"Pussy!" I cried. "Oh, yes! That was one of the words."

Strangers turned to look at us, including a pretty fae girl with curly hair and shiny wings. Her jaw dropped open.

Was she scared of something?

Parker's horns came out and he growled at everyone around us, before hustling us into the alley that went behind Main Street, behind my store. That answered the scared question. He really needed to hide his horns if they scared people that badly. I almost turned to scold Parker, but Migs shoved me up against the brick wall of the alleyway. His hands cushioned my back, so I didn't really slam into the wall, except for my hips. His pelvis pressed into mine hard.

It felt … good.

Somehow, the burning, the intensity, didn't make me want to run screaming that I was on fire, though I was. My nipples tightened and as Migs ground into me, a prickling sensation started up in my pussy. Migs leaned forward and his lips gently brushed over mine. My mind got as bleary and misty as fog.

"Mi amor," he breathed, before he moved to brush his lips along my chin. My head fell back against the wall and that tiny bit of pain was swept away in a sea of pleasure as Migs kissed the rapid pulse in my neck. My eyes lost focus as two more figures moved close.

"What is this?" I whimpered, as the two of them leaned in.

Bar pressed a gentle kiss to my cheek, but Parker reached over and pinched a nipple. A bolt of pleasure shot through me and my pelvis arched up into Migs. "What?" *Is that what nipples do? No wonder Maddie pinched them—*

I couldn't think any more before Parker roughly turned my face to his and plunged his tongue into my mouth. And what started out as a strange sensation turned wonderful as his tongue taught mine what to do. It made me think of things plunging in and out, which reminded me of the vampire in the graveyard, which made me think of mating.

Was this the start of human mating? It was fucking fantastic.

In an ironic twist, it got even more enticing when Barrister growled angrily, "She's my fucking soulmate." And then he grabbed me away from the other two and tried to pin me in by a fire escape.

"Do not—" Migs threat got cut off by Parker's.

"I will fucking ensure your TV only ever plays fucking Barbie cartoons for the rest of your life!" Parker threatened. "We share a soul. She's mine too, dammit."

Bar ignored Parker as his hand reached down and stroked my pussy through my dress and I lost complete track of their argument. Everything in my world became focused on his fingers. They were hard and thick and warm as he stroked up and down the length of my slit. My panties grew soaked at his touch and my hips started to thrust. Yes! I remembered this from the manual. Definitely the start of human mating.

Bar's mouth whispered gruffly in my ear, "You are so fucking precious."

I could only moan in response, my hands flying to his arm and urging him to move his hand faster. My eyelids closed. His fingers lit up pink lights in my brain just like the first time I'd tasted ice cream. His fingers were magic.

Until they were roughly snatched away.

"Wait!" I protested, my eyes fluttering open.

But I didn't see Migs or Parker in front of me.

Instead I saw my brother, John.

He had brown curls, a traditional white choir robe with a gold rope belt, super-sized wings, and a huge frown on his face.

"What are you doing Ruby?"

I'd been sucked through a black hole and spit out the other side. I'd been chained to a dying star and it was exploding all around me. I blinked. English completely left my brain. My mouth opened and closed. But nothing came out.

I'd been worried this body was breaking. Now it was definitely broken.

Because it burned in a way that made me wish it would disintegrate.

Shit. I think they called this embarsement. Embarkment? Em-something. It's awful.

"Who the hell are you?" Migs demanded from behind my brother's spread wings.

"He's a giant feathered cock-block," Parker sneered.

Bar growled, "He's—"

"My brother," I finally found my voice.

John's eyebrows rose. "Not just your brother. Your mentor."

CHAPTER 8

BARRISTER

IT FELT LIKE THE *TEXAS CHAIN SAW MASSACRE* WAS
happening inside my chest. *Well fuck me in the ass with a
feather.* Feeling up Ruby when her brother popped into
the alley—it was not the best way to meet my soulmate's
family for the first time. *Shit.* One look at poor Ruby's
flaming face and I was certain she was about to faint from
humiliation. Better for me to take the brunt of her brother's anger than her. I stepped forward and held out my
hand. "John. It's good to meet you."

The angel turned. As expected, he did not touch my hand.
He glowered, the glow around him turning a dark gold
instead of a bright, sunshiney yellow. He smiled, but it
wasn't in an angelic way. It was in a way that sent chills
down my spine. If he'd been wearing a cowboy hat instead

of a halo, I was pretty sure he'd draw and shoot me. He was the spitting image of a young John Wayne. "Is it?" he asked.

No. No it isn't. Fuck. My eyes darted to Parker and Migs. Migs looked as shell-shocked as when Ruby had hovered in our shop. Dammit. He wasn't gonna be any help.

Parker cleaned his glasses casually on the corner of his shirt, smirking like I was the only one in trouble here. I *was* the only one with his hands on Ruby's pussy ...*Through clothing!* My brain weakly protested, trying to find an out, any out that wasn't going to get me sent straight to the most torturous pit of hell. Parker had told me about it once when we were drunk. It was a combination of the smell of puke, eye surgery performed by possessed puppets, and constant elevator music. He said people broke in less than four hours when they got sent there. I was a sympathy vomiter. One whiff and—no way my eyes would last five minutes in there.

I tried to hide the shudder than went through me when John finally lifted his hand. I'd never tell a soul, but I totally channeled Vol'jin from World of Warcraft in that moment. Utter badass calm with a fucking intimidating goat-skull face. It might have worked because John didn't blast me with lightning. But he also didn't shake my outstretched hand. He left it hanging in midair, making me feel like an idiot as he waited until Ruby took the hand he extended toward her. "Come on, Ruby. You have work to do."

Ruby gave me a weak, half-hearted smile as she slipped

her hand into her brother's. My eyes traced the lines of her body, the tiny swelling on her cheek where a bruise formed from one of her falls. She needed ice. I so badly wanted to hold ice over that spot for her. She licked her lips, the lips that were swollen from all our kisses. From her lips my eyes fell to her plump—

Ruby spoke, drawing my gaze back to her eyes. "Sorry. I don't know what happened with my body back there. I've put in a request to the Mortal Bodies Commission about the boobs, but I'm wondering if my heat sensors have an issue."

Boobs? What issue with the boobs? Her boobs were perfect. My eyes drifted back to them naturally and I had to yank my gaze back up. Heat sensors? Was she talking about her pussy? I clenched my fists to tamp down on the yearning that rose up inside of me at the idea that she might have meant I made her hot. Her eyes were bright, her cheeks still flushed. I wanted to ask what she meant, but I was certain John Wayne would challenge me to a fast draw if I did.

Ruby kept talking. "Anyway, I'll get that fixed. Thanks so much for helping me get back here."

And with that utter nonsense, the girl of my dreams unlocked the back door of her shop and disappeared through it. Her brother stopped in the doorway and turned to face all of us. "You three better run along now. Ruby's on her last strike. She has to get this miracle right or she won't be an angel anymore." He ducked through the door and it started to swing shut.

I ran forward and caught the door before it could fully close. I hadn't fully decided if I was going to give them space or try to follow. But the bomb John had dropped was too much. Ruby? Not be an angel? I gulped and turned to stare at Parker. "What would that mean?"

He pressed his lips together before he spoke in a soft, scared voice. "She'd get booted down to hell. But former angels … ones that don't intend to go there," he shook his head, his hand coming to his mouth. He pulled off his glasses and pinched the top of his nose. I could see how disturbed he looked and that made fear slice open my spine.

Images flashed through my head, horrific images of Ruby being hurt, mocked, tortured. My breath quickened. *No. No fucking way.* I didn't even know if what I was imagining was possible. Or if it would be worse. But no fucking way was I letting my soulmate go there. It didn't matter that we'd just met. Didn't matter that I was some mortal fucking idiot whose only tie to the immortal world was a minor demon who zapped phones for a living. Didn't matter that her brother was probably gonna kick my ass for interfering. I couldn't stand by and let it happen.

I stepped forward, pushing the door farther open. I exchanged an incredulous look with Migs and Parker at my own audacity. I was the fucking friendly dude. The nobody-remembers-him-tomorrow nice guy. The cheat-on-him-and-he'll-take-you-back kinda guy. I wasn't the swashbuckling hero. Fuck. But I threw all that shit aside.

Who I was didn't matter. Because that was yesterday. Before I met Ruby. Before she needed my help. I took another step inside.

Migs was right on my heels. Parker grabbed the door from my hand and swung it open further, gesturing for me to go down the hall. Of course, he *would* let me go first, that demon fucker. If I got fried, there'd just be more Ruby left for him.

I glared for a second but then squared up and nutted up. I was gonna challenge a celestial being. Fuck me. Better to get this over with fast. Like ripping off a band-aid or using a guillotine—whichever it ended up being. I raced into the backroom of Ruby's shoe store. It was a disaster. One set of shelves had been knocked over completely and shoe boxes were scattered randomly across the floor, split open, heels and toes sticking out of crumpled brown paper like bones protruding from dismembered bodies. It looked like a scene out of some warped version of Call of Duty. Like if that game were designed for women, with shoes instead of—fuck—I was seeing carnage everywhere. I was totally expecting to be blasted to smithereens. I overcompensated by bursting into the front room, which was pure white. White walls, white shelves, white register —everything was white except for the pile of boxes that spilled across the floor.

Ruby and John turned, surprised looks on their faces when I said, "We want to help."

John's eyes just narrowed. But Ruby popped around him and said, "Oh, that might be good! Right John? I mean, didn't your humanity rotation end like seventy years ago?"

John rolled his eyes. "Things haven't changed that much."

Migs interjected. "Were you even around for the race to the moon? A ton has happened since then. The invention of the internet. Globalization. Cell phones."

"Trifles," John was dismissive.

Migs's eyes widened in a way that told me he was about to go on a tirade. I took a step toward him and did a low hand gesture, trying to signal him to shut the fuck up. We'd made it in here. We hadn't been murderized. Yet. I wanted to keep it that way. We needed to keep things low key. I needed to atone for groping Ruby in an alley. And we needed to fucking help her out.

Parker didn't help the situation, of course. He made it worse when he added, "Hey, not all trifles. People have invented sex dolls who can take a dick—"

John leaned forward, looking way too interested in that random fact. "I'm on the Universal Reproductive Committee and I've never heard of sex dolls—"

I jumped forward, interjecting. "Look. We're Ruby's … friends." For the first time ever, I hated that word with a passion. Friends. It was such a lie. I hardly even knew her. But she was somehow more important than anyone I'd ever met. I stared into John's brown glare, squaring my shoulders. "We all just want Ruby to succeed. We want to help."

John's eyes narrowed. "Humans know nothing about miracles."

Ruby cleared her throat softly. "They don't know about miracles, but they know about humans. And that's where all my trouble is."

Her face fell and she looked so sad that I wanted to scoop her up and have her sit on the couch wrapped in a blanket while I fed her wine and marshmallows. I had no idea if she even liked marshmallows, but it seemed like an angelic kind of snack.

John shook his head at her. "It's not your trouble, Ruby. It's the human's trouble."

Ruby crossed her arms, her stubbornness lashing out like a snake. "It *is* my trouble if humans don't believe in true love and I don't know that they don't, so I set up a whole miracle for a stupid nonexistent thing like love—"

Her words were like those fucking *Game of Thrones*, Daenerys-gone-crazy, dragon fire. Unexpected and terrifying. I held up a hand. "Wait. Who said we don't believe in true love?" I did. I mean, I wasn't worthy of it. Not with Ruby, anyway. She was so pure and innocent. I was a downright asshole. I hadn't even taken her to dinner before I'd pawed her like a fucking primate. Dammit. I fucking deserved a punch to the nards. But I believed in love—

Ruby snorted. "If I learned anything from last year's disaster, it's that humans don't love the way heaven says they do. Down here, love changes faster than the weather."

"Not true," Migs stepped forward.

Ruby shook her head. Her mouth curved down in a frown; an expression that never should have marred her beautiful face. "Nope. I saw it first-hand. People hop from mate to mate here. Like that game Muriel taught me to play. Checkers?" She played with a strand of hair. "That's why I'm staying away from that whole awful business this Christmas. No love miracles! I'm helping a teenager cope with her sister's death."

John's hand smacked his forehead. "Ruby, that's like a level eight miracle."

She blinked. "Not according to the scroll I was given."

John snapped his fingers and a scroll appeared out of midair. He pulled it open and read aloud, "Level 1: All I Want for Christmas is You: Includes: True Love, Best Friend, Pet. Level 2: Baby Please Come Home for Christmas: Returned Spouse, Child, Parent. Level 3: Oh Santa: Miraculous Gift of Sight, Walking—"

Parker cleared his throat. "Does anyone else notice that these levels sound an awful lot like Mariah Carey Christmas songs?"

Migs just shushed him as Ruby snatched at the scroll. "This is not the version I got!" She leaned against the register and then groaned. "I already submitted all the paperwork for this miracle. Not to mention I promised Maddie that I'd help her sister Holly. Plus, even if I could change, I'd never want a stupid love miracle again anyway. That whole idea of humans having true love is just dog poop."

My heart crumpled like the note I'd sent to Sarah Pattermen in sixth grade. Ruby didn't believe in true love? If she didn't believe in it, how could I ever convince her to love me? At that moment, if the Big Man had come down, I would have had words for him. I mean—*words*. What the fuck was he doing letting me find my soulmate only to find out she'd never love me in return?

CHAPTER 9

RUBY

FOR WHATEVER REASON, BAR SIDLED OVER TO ME AND asked, "Can I pick up in here for you?" He had these sad eyes as he asked, so I nodded. Maybe cleaning cheered him up. I had a soul now, but I still didn't understand why he was sad. What good was a soul if I couldn't understand the reasons for other people's emotions.

Bar reached out to touch my shoulder but stopped short and put his hand down instead. He went over to the boxes of shoes Holly had destroyed the other night and carefully started organizing them. I got a strange feeling watching it, this sadness. For some reason it almost looked like he was punishing himself, but I had no idea why.

John pulled my attention away, of course. "Ruby. Miracle. Rundown. Go."

ANN DENTON

I explained Holly's situation and her sister Maddie to everyone, which just made John run a hand down his face. Seeing that made me cringe a little inside; I'd seen that face far too often. Growing up in his shadow, I'd made a lot of mistakes. And he always had the same reaction. I didn't even need *Harmony's Guide* to understand that human expression. I knew it meant disappointment. He did the same thing no matter what body he was in. Cover his face when he didn't want me to see how I'd failed him. Tears gathered in the corners of my eyes. I did not like disappointing my brother.

"Spirits, Ruby? Ghosts? And a girl who's sad about death —you had to pick the most complicated miracle—" John took a deep breath and smiled at me as he shook his head. He always tried to scold gently. But it didn't make it hurt any less. He sat down on one of my white chairs, pushing aside an open shoe box with his foot. "Girl, it's like you're trying to drive black cattle in the dark."

I stared down at the floor. With my new bit of human soul, I could tell that John was feeling frustrated, but apparently having a soul didn't make English any easier to grasp. I didn't understand the cow reference. Just like I didn't understand most things. It was so fucking frustrating feeling like the stupidest person in the room all the time when I wasn't. Migs walked over and his hand slipped through mine. Could he tell I was at my wit's end? He squeezed my fingers and gave me a smile. It bolstered me a little.

Migs leaned in and whispered in my ear, "He means that you're making work hard for yourself with this miracle."

"I didn't mean to," I murmured back.

"I know, mi corazón, that's why we're here to help." His nose came forward and nuzzled mine. My heart skipped like a little girl down the sidewalk.

I smiled gratefully up at Migs when he pulled back. I realized I loved his blue eyes with their dark lashes. I loved how he somehow knew just what to say.

John cleared his throat. "Umm. Work. Ruby."

I turned to my brother. "All I want is to figure this out and make it work. And then I'll stick to lost pets for the next few decades or whatever. Ugh. Sometimes, the bureaucracy upstairs is so frustrating!"

"Upstairs!" Parker interjected, strolling over behind John to look at my register. He ran a hand down the side. It sparked to life at his touch. "Try working down below. You have scrolls and out-of-date handbooks, but I have daily quotas. You know I have to take out sixteen devices a day? A day! Plus, each month there's a target for generators, fridges, you name it. Silver Springs isn't that big. I have to run to other towns all the time to hit my quotas. Travel, travel, travel. I'm so sick of travel. And I don't even get to stick around to watch people get annoyed half the time. I don't even get to see the hard-earned results of my work."

John shook his head at Parker and turned back around to face me. "This is who you're hanging out with?"

"Hey, we're soulmates. Lay off. I don't like demoning as much as R doesn't like miracling."

My hand flew to my chest. It was so wonderful to hear that I wasn't the only one in the universe who hated their job. I bit down on a grin, because John would definitely not be thrilled to see that.

John scoffed, pointing back over his shoulder. "He doesn't like demoning. Yeah. Right."

I blinked. "Parker wouldn't lie to me." I leaned over and looked at him. "Would you?"

Parker leaned against the table that held the register along with a display of adorable printed socks. "Okay, I don't like *major* demoning. Minor stuff can be fun sometimes. But at the end of the day, it's still a job." Parker crossed his arms over his chest, making his thin shirt spread tight over his sculpted pecs. I temporarily lost track of John's disappointment in me as I stared. I licked my lips.

Of course, Parker noticed. And as John kept talking— coming up with a plan we should follow to achieve this miracle—Parker slowly flicked open the buttons of his collared shirt one by one until I realized I was rubbing my thighs together and nodding absently at whatever John said.

Parker gave me a naughty wink when he pulled his shirt open and traced a nipple.

John snapped his fingers. "Ruby. Focus."

I blinked rapidly and stared at his fingers for a second before focusing on my brother's face as he said, "We need to meet the ghost sister. We'll need to get back some of those things that Holly's parents donated. We'll need to find out where those are."

I nodded. "Sure." I checked the clock. "School's getting out in half an hour. Do we want to meet Holly and figure out where her parents donated everything first?"

John nodded, heading toward the door of my shop.

Bar called out to stop him. "Um. Are you gonna want to change first?" Bar stood up from where he was crouched by a very orderly line of shoes. He gestured at John's robe. "I can lend you some clothes if you need—"

John nodded. "That would be great, thanks."

Bar nodded and walked to the door. Parker held up a hand. "I'm faster. I'll go." He walked toward the front door and turned and leaned against it. "Don't know your sizes for this body, do you John?"

My brother shook his head while he asked, "Did your shirt get ripped?"

Parker didn't answer him, just smiled, before he disappeared as a streak down the street.

Bar returned to the floor and boxed up quite a few shoes. He handed several boxes to Migs and took several boxes himself. "We'll just put these in the back for you."

I nodded and sat on the plush white couch in the show-room. Without my guys here as a buffer, I was certain John would lay it on thick.

He did. John immediately came over and sat down beside me. "You need to distance yourself from these humans, Ruby. And that demon especially. This isn't proper angelic behavior and you know it."

My heart sank. My soul felt like someone had just tossed sand in its eyes. Maybe it wasn't proper angelic behavior. But was I really a proper angel? I mean, I'd agreed to have a spell put on me without really asking what it was. That wasn't proper angelic behavior either. But even though the English thing still caught me up, I felt like I under-stood the guys' emotions a bit more. I felt connected to them in a way I hadn't before. Part of me wanted to connect with them in even more ways—naughty ways like that vampire had connected with that pegasus shifter in the graveyard.

John leaned forward, as if he could tell what I was think-ing, which—technically—he shouldn't be able to do while we were in human bodies because they didn't communi-cate telepathically. "Look, I know you wish that you were in a different assignment. Miracles is a hard division to be in. I'm not gonna lie about that. But I don't want you to fall in with a bad crowd. Two guys and a demon? They're all hormones and trickery. I mean, it can't get much worse."

My stomach fell like a raindrop, plunging down from its happy life in a cloud only to *splat* against the nasty, rocky, pointy ground. John didn't like the guys. My guys. My soulmates.

I was about to respond, but Parker literally rushed back into the showroom at that moment, dropping a huge black garbage bag at our feet. "Here. I grabbed everything in Bar's room for you. Why don't you go upstairs and change and Ruby and I will grab everyone coffee? The guys and I didn't get our morning jolt and I'm sure we could all use it."

John started to protest, but Parker grabbed me around the waist, picked me up, and ran out the door and down the street before my brother could say another word. Parker stopped seconds later in front of Jewels Café. He set me down on the sidewalk outside the busy little shop and ushered me into the line, his hand on the small of my back just like I saw a man doing to his wife in front of him.

"What would you like, gorgeo—"

"Hey, do I know you?" A guy with close-cropped brown hair walked up to Parker and squinted. "I've seen you in here before." The guy wore a brown leather bomber jacket and had a laptop case slung over his shoulder.

Next to me, Parker shook his head, a little too frantically. I felt proud of myself that I recognized the over-shaking technique as odd. But then I realized Parker was nervous. His hand clutched at the back of my dress. Why was he nervous?

I extended my hand to greet the guy in front of us. "Hi. I'm Ruby." I smiled.

The guy smiled in return. He didn't seem threatening. He seemed kind of sweet. I didn't get any alpha/predator vibes from him at all. But when his gaze turned back to Parker, it was flat, lacking any of the warmth he'd shared with me. "I don't think it's a good idea for you to keep coming here man. I'm pretty sure you're the reason my computer died last week." He arched a brow at Parker.

"It wasn't me," Parker denied. But even as he said that, a woman jabbering on her cell phone suddenly stopped and looked at her screen. "Dammit."

All of us turned to look at her as she tapped her fake nails repeatedly against the phone screen and heaved a frustrated sigh.

"Not you, huh?"

"Look, I'm just trying to get my girl some coffee. Please. I won't come back after this. Look. Here." Parker reached into his jacket and pulled out a carrot. He offered it to the other man.

Were carrots a form of bribery on earth? I thought people only wanted those plastic cards or paper bills. Stupid *Harmony*.

"You know there's a grocery store just down the street, right?" The man scowled as a pretty blonde woman in an apron walked over to us. She looked familiar. I think she'd been in my shop before.

"Chase, honey, I think you're holding up the line." She leaned fondly on Chase's shoulder and his hand went to cover hers in a gesture that made me pine. I wanted that. I'd thought I'd felt it for a second when Parker's hand had been on my spine. But, was I wrong? Was John right? Was I just getting tricked?

"Is that a *carrot*?" the blonde woman raised an eyebrow as she looked from Chase to Parker and back again.

"Apparently," Chase scowled at Parker. "Not all bunny shifters like carrots, you know."

"Are you sure?" The blonde looked up at him innocently.

I felt like I was missing something. Since when did bunnies not like carrots?

"Amber, sweetheart, you know—" Chase said.

"I do," Amber smirked. "But this man is offering you *his carrot …*"

My eyes darted between the two as Chase's eyes widened and he held up his hands and made a giant X in the air with them. Was this one of those situations where people had gone and changed the meaning of a word? Dammit!

"No. Just no," Chase said.

"I can clearly see it right there." Amber nudged her chin toward the carrot.

"I can too," I jumped into the conversation. "It's a pretty big carrot. It looks nice and crisp. I bet it tastes delicious."

Amber turned to us, her eyes sparkling with mischief. "Sorry. Just had to pester him." She grabbed the carrot out of Parker's hand. "Grab your coffees on the house." She turned to Chase. "You. Come with me." She looped her arm around his. "We need to have a talk about you digging in other people's gardens." She led him off, taking a bite out of Parker's carrot as they walked through the door to the kitchen.

Chase's voice drifted back to us as he told Amber, "I have a pretty delicious carrot too. Wanna taste?" Before the door swung shut, I saw Chase's hand swat Amber's ass. Her giggle floated back to us. What an odd couple. Fighting in public was obviously some kind of turn on for them. Though why they'd fight over vegetables, I had no idea.

We put in our order. As we waited, Parker turned to face me.

"So ... I know that I'm the sticking point here. Being what I am," his mouth quirked up to the side, but I could tell he wasn't happy. I could feel how he was sad, frustrated, and regretful all at once. It was almost overwhelming, knowing he felt all those things. Knowing that he felt all those things because of the connection we had. Did he want to break it? My chest curled up into a tight little ball at that thought.

But Parker reached out and took my hand gently. "I can't lie about who or what I am. But, this—" he gestured between us, where the emotion sat thick as whipped cream on top of hot chocolate. "It's worth things getting a little weird sometimes, right? It's worth having to share with Migs and Bar and getting over the differences and morality quibbles to feel *this*, right?"

He bit his lip as he looked at me. Behind him, a register sparked, making the teenage girl working it jump back and shriek.

"Shit," he muttered. "I didn't mean to do that."

Parker moved me farther down the counter toward the napkin holders, so that he was away from electronics. His fingers wove through mine and he held our hands up in front of us, like he was creating a bridge between us, his soul to mine. I could feel the intensity of his words when he said, "Ruby, you haven't said anything." He pressed his lips together and closed his eyes. "If you're gonna say no, do it now. Please. Before I can become even more attached."

I froze. The idea of ending things felt ... wrong. It felt like trying to walk on a cloud upside down. Or trying to breathe water in this human body. It felt unnatural. But Parker was a demon. A hot demon, yes. A sneaky, naughty demon kinky enough to tempt me even when my brother was in the room. But he was a demon. I was an angel.

"How do you really feel about evil?" I asked.

His eyes opened and he gave me a soft smile. "I'm in the tech division by choice. Anything darker turns my stomach."

I worried my lip. "And what do you think about angels?"

"Mostly uptight bastards who wouldn't know how to take a joke if it smacked them in the ass. But, some angels … aren't like the others." He raised our linked fingers and kissed the back of my hand.

The barista called out our order, but Parker didn't move. He straightened and his eyes studied mine as he waited anxiously for my answer.

I stood up on my tiptoes and pressed my lips to Parker's. And it felt good. The kiss felt like a sneeze that I'd been holding in that just *needed* to come out, like something I'd been holding back that needed to be free. It felt as exciting as the first moment I opened a brand-new scroll on a brand-new world. It felt like taking that first cold sip of water after flying too close to the sun. It felt so good that my toes tingled.

The lights flickered and went out. All around us people groaned.

"Oops," Parker shrugged, his eyes twinkling as he pulled away. He laughed softly.

Then I laughed.

Then he laughed.

We grabbed our coffees and wove our way through a crowd of shadows to the door, laughing. Parker and I both chuckled out of excitement and fear.

I'd just agreed to some kind of relationship with a demon.

My brother's warning went through my head again as

Parker led the way down the street. My demon was so happy that every single human we passed ended up stopping mid-stride and cursing their dead cell phone. I was happy he was happy. I was happy that I was happy.

But human emotions were tricky things. Happiness didn't equate to goodness. Even if we were happy together, it didn't mean we were good together.

The question sat inside me like a lump of coal in a Christmas stocking. Who should I believe? My brother or a demon?

CHAPTER 10

Migs

I HAD TO BITE MY TONGUE, WHICH WAS INCREDIBLY HARD for me. But one doesn't make fun of an angel. Mi abuela would come back and haunt me if she knew I had done that. And now that I knew ghosts were real, and that was actually a possibility ... I bit down on my lower lip, determined to keep quiet.

But John looked ridiculous. Completely fucking ridiculous.

Bar's normal pants hadn't fit John. But thoughtful demon that he was, Parker had apparently put Bar's cosplay outfits in the trash bag too. So, John was wearing some bright blue Mario Brothers overalls from an outfit Bar had made a few years back. But he wore the overalls with an ugly Christmas sweater Bar had that happened to have

Thor's hammer on the front. Then, he paired the outfit with some men's shoes from the backroom of Ruby's store. We'd tried to get him to wear tennis shoes, but he'd insisted on slippers because they were so much softer.

"Those won't really work in a graveyard—" I'd said.

"Those are gonna get torn up," Bar had stated.

"All those other contraptions are awful on the feet. Even worse than I remember," John had argued as he'd pulled on eggplant-purple fuzzy slippers.

He was intending to lead us to the high school. I couldn't let that happen. No way a teenage girl was gonna listen to us if clown-man here tried to talk. Holly would run the other direction. And that wouldn't help Ruby one bit.

Bar kept trying to engage John in regular conversation, but John was being a little CIA about it all.

"My last assignment was confidential. I can't discuss it with mortals."

Ruby and Parker got back with coffee as John said that. And my chest purred like a contented cat, seeing her again.

Of course, she just looked quizzically at John and asked, "Weren't you sent out on that tentacle clean up committee?"

John sputtered, his face going red.

"Tentacles?" Bar asked.

Ruby giggled as she passed around our coffees. The sound was as invigorating as coffee itself—warm and energizing. "Yes. Some bright mind had the idea to give an alien species of women tentacles. Well, I'll give you one guess what they did with them. Procreation nearly halted on the planet."

The guys and I all stopped. Bar looked kind of turned on by the thought. I would have to see pictures of the alien species before I got the same idea. If aliens actually looked like the movie *Alien*, or *E.T.* or *Men In Black*—basically, if aliens looked anything like they did in movies—I didn't give a damn what those females did with their tentacles. More power to them.

Parker's hand brushed Ruby's back as he passed her, and she gave him one of those shy, sweet glances that new couples often give. I saw Bar tense up next to me, so I walked over to him. I leaned in. "Hey, dude."

Bar looked over at me and gave me a look. I could tell just by the expression on his face that he was jealous and annoyed and trying to hide it. I couldn't do anything about how he felt about Parker or me and our connection to Ruby. Not yet anyway. But I could give him a shot at a little alone time with Ruby so that maybe he'd feel more confident. He'd always been the most insecure of us. I leaned close to him and jabbed a thumb in John's direction as the angel downed some coffee. "John can't go to the high school like this. I mean—look at him."

Bar nodded.

"We're gonna take two Ubers. You go in the one with Ruby. Parker and I will go with John."

Bar looked at me, understanding crossing his face. He gave me a small smile before he nodded and whipped out his phone, ordering his ride as I did the same.

When the cars came, I slipped the front driver a twenty to take off like a bat out of hell once Ruby and Bar were in the backseat. Then Parker and I took up the backseat of the second car, forcing John to sit next to the Uber driver.

Parker read over the text I sent him. He glanced up at me and gave a quick nod when he finished. Then he waved his hand, and the map on the driver's phone flickered. Our route changed to be the most roundabout route to the high school you'd ever seen. John was too busy touching buttons up front to notice.

"What's this do?" he asked, as he pushed a button to spring open the change holder. Inside, there wasn't change. There were little dime bags. I didn't know of what. I didn't want to know. I stared out the window and pretended not to notice as the driver hurriedly shoved the drawer closed.

"Hands off, you bumble fuck. This is a ride, it ain't *your* ride."

Well, that took off two stars at least.

Parker stretched the seatbelt as far as it would go and leaned between them. "So, John, tell me: what do you think about the objectification of angels?"

"WHAT?" John turned in his seat and I realized he hadn't put on a seatbelt. He crouched near the glove compartment as he said, "What are you talking about?" His eyes narrowed on Parker as if any objectification was Parker's fault.

I felt lost for a second. I had no idea what Parker was thinking. "Do you mean like kitch?" I asked. "Like how they sell angel magnets or night lights?"

Parker shook his head and his fingers flew across his phone. "No. Like this."

He held up his phone, showing us a photo of a Victoria Secret model walking down a runway.

John's reaction was classic horror movie shit. His hand flew to his chest and his gasp almost made our driver swerve into a fire hydrant.

"Fuck!" said our driver.

"Lightning bolts!" said John.

I was pretty certain they both meant the same thing.

John grabbed onto the phone and stared. "Who's doing this? Stripping angels of clothing and ..." he shook his head. "This is just as bad as those Renaissance perverts painting us naked on church ceilings—HOW HAS THIS NOT MADE IT UP TO THE ANGELIC PROPAGANDA COMMITTEE?"

Suddenly, John's body melted into a ball of light and

winked out of existence, his borrowed clothes falling to his seat, his slippers empty on the car floorboards.

Our driver screeched to a halt. "Holy shit balls. Fuck. I knew I shouldn't have taken those 'shrooms before this shift. Fuck."

Parker and I exchanged a look. We were surrounded by crazies. We climbed out of the car.

I gathered up John's clothes before the Uber driver took off, tires smoking and screeching.

Parker and I walked to Stone Hill High.

When we got there, school was just letting out.

Girls who were dressed for summer at the beach instead of winter weather poured out the front doors in short skirts. I rolled my eyes. Teenage girls had never made sense to me. Not when I was a teenager and not now.

My eyes scanned the front lawn and spotted Ruby and Bar, his arm slung around her shoulders, a single yellow flower in her hands.

I fought the urge to roll my eyes. Of course, he'd probably stopped the car to run over and grab that at a convenience store or something.

Parker and I strolled over to them only to find them chewing on Red Vine licorice as they looked through the crowd for Holly.

"Where's John?" Ruby asked as soon as they spotted us.

I didn't answer. The sight of Ruby sucking on that strand of licorice did things to me. Serious things.

Parker didn't notice her fellating the candy and just reached over and grabbed a vine from the bag in Bar's hand. "Your bro had to go bring something to a committee or something. He'll be back soon, I'm sure." Then, the demon had to stir the shit, like always. "You know, yellow flowers are supposed to be for friendship," he nodded toward the sunflower in Ruby's hands.

Bar's face reddened. "That's not true."

Parker shook his head. "Flower language. It's a thing. We used to have a whole division to help fuck it up and send mixed messages until red roses started dominating the market." Parker leaned casually against a tree, twirling his licorice.

I punched his shoulder. "Dude. Shut up." I glanced mean-ingfully over at Bar, who was trying to nut up and tell Ruby his flower didn't mean friendship.

Parker rolled his eyes but shut his mouth.

"I thought flowers were part of mating rituals down here," Ruby said, blinking up at Bar.

His face reddened like a beet. "Yeah, um, they are."

Her smile and his resulting awkwardness were almost painful to watch. When Bar was confident, he was hilari-ous, fun to be around. But when he got shy or felt insecure, it was like a puppet master took over his body. He got all spastic and jerky and awkward.

Thank fuck Holly appeared, or the girl I assumed was Holly—based on the death glare she gave us as she marched over. The blonde girl was prettier than most, even if she did have a perpetual pouty look about her. She had the air of a popular girl, which I knew made Bar cringe. I didn't mind as much, but Parker just smiled lazily from his spot against the tree.

Ruby waved enthusiastically.

I walked toward the sweet angel and caught her hand in mine, kissing it. "Ruby, corazón, teenagers generally like to pretend adults don't exist. Maybe less waving, huh?"

Ruby's eyes widened. "Oh, right. Yes. Sure." She put down her hand and waited until Holly got close enough to hiss at us.

"What the fuck? What are you doing here?" Holly hissed.

I was pissed she was being that rude to Ruby.

Ruby didn't seem to notice. She gave the girl a bright smile. "Hi, Holly. These are my soulma—"

I interrupted. "We're Ruby's friends. We thought you might want some help searching the thrift stores for your sister's clothes."

Holly stopped walking, shocked.

And then she dropped her book bag and walked forward to give Ruby a hug.

The tears that misted in Ruby's eyes were the most beautiful sight I'd ever seen.

And I decided right then and there that I'd do whatever it took to make her happy.

Anything.

CHAPTER 11

Ruby

We were at the second thrift store when Holly's ex texted her.

"My ex, Joe, thinks he's a total GOAT," Holly rolled her eyes as she shoved her phone into her pocket and started aggressively shoving aside shirts on the rack.

"He thinks he's a farm animal?" I asked. That sounded like a serious problem. It was probably a good thing they stopped dating.

"No. Greatest of All Time. It's an acronym, Ruby. Sometimes, I swear," Holly rolled her eyes as she stomped off to look in another area.

Apparently, once again, my ignorance was annoying. *Well,*

get in line, Holly. It's not just annoying to you. It's pretty fucking annoying to me, too, I thought as I shoved a vintage pink t-shirt aside.

My eyes drifted up to find Miguel's. He exchanged a sympathetic look with me. *Teenagers. English. Miracles. Ugh.*

Parker slid a hand over my shoulder and tickled the back of my neck with his fingertips before saying, "I got this one, sweetheart."

My heart did one of those shy, happy swivels, the kind where you link your hands in front of you and sway your shoulders side to side as you smile. He called me sweetheart. That, I could understand.

Less than two minutes later, Parker had Holly laughing up a storm. They walked back toward us; heads buried in Holly's phone. Then she held it up like a trophy. "Look! Parker somehow hacked Joe's phone. Now everything he posts in Insta comes out in German!"

The two of them doubled over in laughter.

Holly laughed until she was gasping. "Oh, it hurts!"

I rushed over. "Do you need a doctor? How did he hurt you?"

Holly waved me off.

Parker swiped at his eyes and smiled. "She's just laughed so hard her stomach hurts."

"Oh," I blinked. I didn't know laughter could have negative consequences. *Note to self, human bodies cannot handle large amounts of laughter.*

Even though it apparently caused her some pain, it was good to see Holly laugh, even if it wasn't for the nicest reason. Baby steps back to normal—that's what the miracle guide said anyway. Holly was typically rolling her eyes at me and not laughing. But after Parker's little prank, she smiled nearly the entire rest of our search.

Pride swelled in my chest at Parker. I didn't know if he'd meant to do something good. But he had. And that little connection between our souls sizzled as a result. I could feel it. And I could see the little orange flickers of soul around his heart were bigger and stronger than before.

When the others wandered to the shoe section, I gave him a soft kiss on the neck to thank him.

He looked down at me, surprised. "What was that for?"

"For being sweet." I smiled, then backtracked. "I've seen couples do it. But, um … I'm sorry. If you don't want my body parts to touch yours … I probably should have asked first."

Parker swung his arm around my shoulders and leaned down. He kissed my neck in return, then whispered, "Your body parts can touch mine any time you want."

For some reason, those words made my private area catch fire. I had to scurry away to the ladies' room to make sure there wasn't any actual combustion going on down there.

Luckily, it looked normal. So maybe too many sweet words did to my body what too much laughter did to Holly's—made it malfunction.

Holly's good mood lasted all night. She even smiled at Bar, who came up with ridiculous outfit combinations, though she rolled her eyes when she found out he was into cosplay.

"Dude, that's so extra. And not in a good way," she said when Bar tried on a mauve top hat that he said he could use to make a Mad Hatter costume.

Bar bought it anyway, because I told him that the color looked good with his skin, which it did, before his cheeks and neck turned bright red.

When the store closed at eight, we left—without finding anything that had belonged to Maddie—and grabbed a slice of pizza, before the guys called an uber van. We dropped off Holly.

She actually waved goodbye as she walked to the front door, which her mom opened for her.

I was feeling pretty good about this assignment, and life, and even earth, when all the guys turned to look at me expectantly.

Nervous flutters started in my stomach. Shoot. Just when I'd thought everything was good, clearly it wasn't. Clearly, I was missing something, like always. "What?"

The driver turned and looked at me. "Where do you want to go?"

Three stares burned through me like the laser guns my angel legion had used in the Kuhaulan War in the Sombrero Galaxy. "Um …"

Bar grabbed my hand and leaned forward. "If you come back to our place, you don't have to do anything."

I scrunched my brow. That made zero sense. "Why would I want to go to your place if we're not gonna do anything?"

Migs leaned over from the seat on the other side of me and his hot, warm breath on my ear sent tingles to all the right places. All the mating places. Migs whispered, "He means, you don't have to do anything sexual. We can just get to know one another better. Maybe play a game."

My heart beat triple time. They wanted me to go back to their apartment. "Okay," I said shyly.

Migs lips immediately went to the lobe of my ear as Bar's hand clamped down on mine.

Bar leaned forward and pushed Migs back in his seat. "She said okay to heading back to our place, not to kissing. We haven't worked out the rules for any of that yet."

"Rules? There are more rules?" I asked, trying not to whine. Earth had way too many rules.

"He means about the three of us sharing you," Parker clarified.

The uber driver started coughing up front. Hard.

I leaned forward, concerned. "Do you need a cough drop? I might have something in my purse."

The man beat on his chest as he pulled up to the guy's apartment building. He sucked in air, gasping as he said, "Nope. Nope. I'm good."

"Okay, well thank you for driving us," I waved at the driver as Bar helped me out of the van and then slid an arm around my waist. Parker slid an arm around my shoulders as Migs unlocked the door. Bar pushed Parker's arm off.

"Dude," Parker said.

"Dude," Bar said.

I shrugged out of both of their holds as they stared into one another's eyes. I could sense tension between them, but I wasn't quite certain why. What had made them angry? Had I done something wrong? Again?

I looked away, trying to decide what I might have done. I realized the Uber driver was still parked in his van, staring at all of us as his shoulder spasmed oddly.

I tapped Bar on the shoulder. "I think that man might be having a seizure!"

Bar and Parker turned to look at the driver.

"It's illegal to jerk off in public, you fuckwad!" Parker shouted, causing people on the street to turn and look at the man in the van, who started up the engine, flipped Parker off, and then drove away.

So, I guess it wasn't a seizure then. The driver's body had been working just fine. I sighed. Yet another thing in this stupid world I didn't get.

I almost asked what jerking off was, but Parker ended up saying, "I can't believe he was stroking his dick in public."

Oh. Well, that explained the somewhat pained look on the guy's face then. Mating and seizure faces did look a lot alike. At least they did in the handbooks I'd studied.

Bar hustled me inside, arms around me. "I'm so sorry, Ruby. I'm so sorry."

"Why?" I asked him. He looked so upset. I could tell whatever the driver had done bothered him.

"Because you shouldn't be exposed to assholes like that."

"People who perform mating rituals in public?" I asked as Bar led me to their leather couch and Migs handed me a glass of red wine. Their place was nice—clean, full of leather. They even had a brown rug on their wooden floor. Of course, it wasn't as soft as my rug. But their human feet probably weren't as sensitive to the stupid ground as mine.

I studied Bar's furrowed brow as I asked, "But, didn't we do the same thing earlier today? A mating ritual in the alley?" My stomach tightened as I remembered it, and a delicious shiver traveled down my spine. Remembering the feel of their mouths and hands on me shot sparks through my body. Thinking about it made me wish it was happening all over again. I wriggled on the couch, pressing my knees together. As my thighs touched, I realized that my panties were damp.

Bar sat down on one side of me. Migs sat on the other. I looked back and forth between them as they smiled at me. I swallowed hard, anticipation building in my stomach like steam until I wanted to scream. I felt desperate for them to touch me. But they didn't.

Parker closed the apartment door and locked it, before coming to stand behind me. His hand drifted over the back of my neck before Bar's glare had him pulling away.

"Yes, and I want to apologize for what happened in the alley," Bar said softly. "We should never have taken things that far. You deserve better. So much better."

My stomach fell, and all the naughty mating visions I'd had in my head dissolved. "What's better than mating?" I asked, honestly confused. I thought mating was the ultimate human expression of connection.

Bar swallowed hard next to me.

Parker took a seat in a leather armchair near us as he said, "Nothing is better than mating. Especially with your *soulmate*." He put a lot of emphasis on that last word before he leaned over to the glass coffee table, grabbed the bottle of wine that Migs had set down there, and took a swig.

If nothing was better than mating, then why didn't they

want to mate with me? Didn't they call me their soulmate? It had mate in the word. Didn't that mean we were supposed to mate? Did they not want me? Did they wish Amethyst hadn't given me this little bit of soul?

My heart snapped like a broken harp string. It hurt. Deep inside it hurt to know my mates rejected me. And then I realized, they might not just reject me, they might resent me.

I turned to Migs. "I'm so sorry I took your soul without asking." My hands reached for his and I clasped them, pleading for forgiveness. "I don't know of a way to give it back."

Migs took one of my hands and kissed the back, saying softly, "Corazón, I don't want it back. I love our connection. We all do."

Bar huffed at that.

Migs glared at his friend before reaching out to stroke my hair. "Barrister isn't saying he doesn't want to mate. He wants to. We all want to—"

Barrister groaned and his hand slid to my thigh, squeezing it possessively at Miguel's words.

Migs gave Bar a hard stare and the other man's hands retreated.

"But if you want to, then why aren't we?" I wasn't certain what lying felt like. But it didn't seem possible that they could be telling the truth. "My body wants you guys." I placed Migs hand over my breast so he could feel how fast my heart was beating, how hard my nipple had grown. If their bodies felt the same things; if they had the same mating instincts, how could they resist? Unless they were lying.

Migs groaned as he pulled his hand away from my breast, leaving it aching for his touch.

Barrister spoke and I turned to look at him. "We want to ensure you know you're respected, well-treated, liked for the person you are and not just this amazing body—" His eyes traveled down my figure in a way that left no doubt he was feeling the urge to mate, too. His dick was hard, the outline clearly visible through his pants.

He did want to mate. I glanced at Migs and Parker, whose shafts were also thick and ready. They all wanted to mate if their dicks were any indication.

But, perhaps in this realm, the men needed more of a mating dance to convince them to move forward? Maybe the alleyway had been too rushed? Maybe they needed reassurance or proof that I would be a good mate? Maybe they were like the males in the avian community in the Cartwheel galaxy who only mated with a female after she built them a nest. But they already had a nest. Ugh. I needed some kind of directions! The problem was that I didn't trust *Harmony's Guide* anymore. I had no clue what kind of mating dance these guys would want me to do. Fucking shooting stars! This was frustrating. But I wanted to mate with them. My body and soul demanded it. I'd have to swallow my pride and ask what kind of pre-mating requirements they had.

"If you aren't ready to mate, what do you want to do?" My eyes traveled over each one of them.

Bar cleared his throat, his neck going a bit red as he asked, "Have you ever heard of *Call of Duty*?"

CHAPTER 12

PARKER

IT TOOK HER AN HOUR TO LEARN THE CONTROLS, BUT RUBY fucking annihilated us after that. She was amazing, a goddess of death. And the righteous fury that shone in her eyes as she wore a headset and screamed, "Die you hellspawn! Die!" was so goddamned hot. I had to go to the bathroom to jerk off more than once.

At ten, we all walked Ruby back to her apartment above The Perfect Fit. Those gorgeous wings of hers came out and Migs had his hands all over them, complimenting their softness. I ached to stroke them, but I resisted until she gave each one of us a goodnight kiss. When I got mine, I let a finger trail over her wings as my tongue plundered her mouth. Migs was right, her wings were soft. But they also seemed to be an erogenous zone. I trailed my fingers over them, teasing her until I heard a little moan.

When I pulled back, her hooded eyes and dark breathing nearly made me push her inside.

Until the door swung open behind her and the blonde witch who'd chased me down the street from coffee shop said, "Ruby, what the fuck! I've been searching everywhere for you. I finally gave up and used my key!"

Ohh, she was pissed.

Ruby didn't seem too perturbed though because she just said, "Amethyst, hi. Meet my soulmates."

Amethyst shook her head and grabbed Ruby's hand, shoving a scroll into it.

Ruby unrolled it. "What's this?"

Amethyst responded, "I dunno. It just fell on my head."

Ruby unrolled the scroll. "Oh! It's that boob reduction, I applied for! They've granted—"

I yanked that scroll out of her hand and threw it as far as I could. I wished at that moment that I was a fire demon and I could have lit that shit paper on fire. "You do *not* need a boob reduction."

Ruby's eyebrows flew up. "I don't?"

Migs and Bar backed me up, adamantly shaking their

heads. If Amethyst hadn't been there, I might have backed Ruby up against the wall and showed her how hot her breasts were.

"But I fall. All the time," Ruby argued, twisting a lock of that gorgeous dark brown hair around her finger. "My balance is horrible."

"Did you fall at all tonight?" I asked.

"Well … no."

"We won't let you fall, Ruby," Bar promised.

Amethyst cleared her throat. "Alright, *strangers*. Well, I think it's time you two and kidnapper over there—" she pointed at me, "head on home."

It was safe to say I'd made a pretty bad impression on her.

"We'll be back in the morning, beautiful," Bar said. "We'll go to the other thrift shops on the list. It's Saturday, they'll be open early."

Ruby nodded, one of her cute, over-enthusiastic, made-me-want-to-squeeze-the-shit-out-of-her smiles lighting up her face. I clamped my hands and shoved them into my jacket pockets. I doubted Amethyst would appreciate if I grabbed Ruby right now and repeated this morning's performance, even if every part of me just wanted to grab my soulmate and take her away.

I blew out a deep breath and yanked on the guys. We needed to go home. And we needed to talk.

Because Ruby was here.

Our soulmate was fucking here. We'd found her. This was happening. She was happening.

To all of us.

We were only two steps into the apartment when Migs said, "We're fucked."

He went and got three shot glasses. And the three of us each took shots of tequila until we were drunk enough to have an honest conversation about feelings and shit.

Migs slammed his shot glass down onto our countertop so hard that the glass chipped. "Fuck," he tossed it in the trash as he said, "We have to find a way to share."

Bar shook his head. "That would be like cheating." And he walked off to his room without another word.

"Does that mean he's out?" Migs asked.

"You'd know better than me."

Migs shook his head. "He'd back out because he thought it was honorable. He'd live miserable, just pining for her, if we let him."

I shrugged, helping myself to a swig from the bottle. "Well, go talk to him."

Migs shook his head. "You go talk to him."

"I'm more likely to piss him off!" I argued. And maybe get

pissed in return and fry his laptop, which wouldn't help matters.

"You share a fucking soul, you conchudo."

"Pussy? Dude, that's harsh."

Migs turned and walked to the bathroom, slamming the door shut. He yelled through it. "I gotta shit."

Fucker. He was probably lying. But his shits took hours. And Bar was ten minutes from sleep. The man couldn't handle alcohol. Dammit all.

I would have put it off, but that would mean it would take even longer to work shit out with Ruby. Which meant keeping my hands off her. And I didn't want to do that.

Fuck. I waved a hand, letting my horns and tail show. This conversation was gonna take all my concentration. There wouldn't be any room left for magic. I ran a hand over my forehead and scratched the base of one of my horns. *Just do it, Parker,* I coached myself.

I marched down the hall, threw open the door to Bar's room and said, "She's as much mine as she is yours. I mean, dude, why do you think I jumped at the chance to get a little bit of your soul?"

Bar had changed into workout gear and was doing pushups when I came in. He stopped, sitting on the floor, and looked at me blandly. "Because you're a demon." Bar shook his head as if he were stating the obvious. Which he was. Kinda.

"But why do demons want souls?" I prompted.

"To get people to go to hell."

"That's just bad press," I waved an arm nonchalantly as I met my lie quota for the day. I typically tried to meet it by lying to strangers. A quick, "Oh, you look so good in that shirt!" or two. But we'd been together all day, so I hadn't had a chance to get out and hit those quotas. And to fly under the radar, I *had* to meet some.

I cleared my throat. The next words out of my mouth weren't a lie. They were pure truth. "Demons want souls—and angels are strictly forbidden from getting them—because the soul is a little piece of divinity. It's shredded and divided between two or more people and the connection when they find one another … it's the most profound experience that exists."

Bar's eyebrows lowered as he studied me. He got up and grabbed an orange nerf ball from a basket on his desk. He tossed it at my chest. "You're fucking with me, right?"

I caught the ball and tossed it back at him with a gentle arc. "Don't you feel that connection with Ruby?"

Bar stared at the ball and nodded.

And then the drunk part of me took over. I was glad, but also mortified when it said, "Trust me when I say that I've existed for nearly a millenium. There's nothing better than what I feel right now."

Bar's head went from side to side as if he partially agreed

with my words. "That part I can believe— But taking my soul—that's bullshit. You're recruiting for the dark side, Vadar."

Shit. I could feel the tic mark I'd gotten for the lie get erased inside my head, where the demonic tally system was implanted. "Fine. Fucker. That shirt makes you look like a preschooler." Bar's shirt actually showed off his sculpted torso. The lie quota in my head got scratched off again as I threw the nerf ball and it bounced off the side of Bar's head.

"Your dick looks like a preschooler's," Bar retorted, going to the pull-up bar he'd installed on his walk-in closet door.

"Glad to hear you've been staring at it," I winked.

He laughed, dropping from the bar. "Get out of my room, fucker." He pointed.

"In a sec," I leaned against the door, heart pounding as I pressed for what I wanted. Stupid alcohol. Making me desperate and shit. Was it the alcohol? Or just Ruby? "I need to hear you say it first. You've been kind of a dick about it. And I get it. Puritanical monogamy culture and all that. But I need to hear you say that you're cool with sharing Ruby. Because this connection is all of us, man."

Bar's face scrunched up tight. I knew that the shit that went down with Darlene had hit him hard. The idea of sharing wasn't natural to him. But the idea that the girl would pick someone else … maybe that's the part of him I needed to reassure.

I tilted my head to the side and said, "You know she won't choose any of us. Right? She'd never force any of us or pick one over the other. She's a fucking angel, dude. She won't have a favorite. It would rip her bit of soul up to hurt us."

Bar chewed his lip and turned away. He popped back up on the bar, facing away from me as he did a set of twenty pull ups.

I waited, unmoving. Inside, I was a coiled spring. I was full of tension and ready to pop. But outside, I was calm. Because Bar didn't need to feel attacked or pressured. I needed him to truly, honestly be good with this. I didn't lie to myself. Stealing Ruby would appeal to that dark part of me. But sharing her—the idea of that made my heart and dick swell to the size of goddamned blimps. That was fucking better.

But maybe he was okay with sharing her with Migs. Maybe it was me he had a problem with. I mean, he and Migs were tight. Migs probably would have gotten him on board with sharing Ruby in two seconds flat. So why hadn't he come in here? Why'd he send me? Unless I was the problem. Unless the problem was sharing Ruby with me. Tainting her with me.

It felt like someone had taken a can opener to my heart and just cut out a big jagged circle.

Fuck. That was it. I'm the problem.

I pictured Ruby's face. Those dark curls and eyes just begging to be taught what naughty was. Her soft lips. That angry look she got. How sweet her laugh was when she'd rocked *Call of Duty* and high-fived us all. She was a damn angel. How could I force her or the guys to be contaminated by me? Not for the first time, I fucking hated my own existence. I'd thought that I wanted to burn up and drift away like ash on the wind when I'd helped the Yaarkin destroy the planet Alza. But now, I wished I'd never even existed. It would be better than giving Ruby up.

But that's what you have to do, dickwad, I told myself as Bar finished his reps and turned to face me.

His expression was serious. So, I spoke before he could.

"You can have your soul back if I'm the problem. I don't want to do anything that would get in the way of her happiness." Fuck me. Saying that hurt. It fucking literally set my nerve endings on fire. I could feel all the tic marks in my head, all the quotas I'd met that day, get erased. My boss's round, red face appeared behind my eyes, his horns were flaming which meant he was ready to rage at me—but somehow, a white veil descended between us. And I couldn't hear him. Couldn't see him. The burning in my limbs subsided. But the nervous energy didn't. I still felt like I was standing on the edge of a cliff, waiting for Bar to push me over.

Bar's face was shocked. His jaw hung so low I thought it might have disconnected.

I waited, hands curling into fists, heart thrumming.

He opened his mouth and I prepared myself to run. Out the door, out of this town, around the world. I'd need to get away after.

But Bar shocked me when he said, "If you'd do that for her, then you deserve her too, man."

The air left my lungs and stupid fucking tears filled my eyes. "What?"

"You're right," Bar said. "She's not some normal girl. She's our soulmate."

Dammit all to hell if my insides didn't feel like the end of one of those Hallmark movies. All pure and joyful and shit. This couldn't be happening. I was a demon. Good things *couldn't* happen to me. By their very definition, good things couldn't happen.

But Bar came forward and slung an arm across my shoulders. He gave me a bro nod, the kind he usually only gave to Migs. Fuck.

He was letting me keep his soul. He was sharing Ruby. I had a soul and a soulmate and a best friend. Two best friends. I felt like I was on top of the world. That feeling lasted all night. It lasted all morning, as the guys and I got up early, energized because Migs said he'd looked online and found a new hip consignment shop that was just opening up. So, we got dressed—the guys bundled up against the early morning chill, but I wore a grey suit I knew drove the women mad. I was celebrating, and demons ran hot anyway. And I wanted Ruby's eyes to devour me like they had yesterday at the coffee shop.

We detoured to see if the owner, a very sweet woman in her forties, (who seemed tickled to have the attention of a trio of guys in their twenties) might let us look at her start up merchandise for some intense comicon costumes.

"Sure, sweetie," she'd pinched Bar's cheek and he'd just smiled in return.

After five minutes, I spotted a purple scarf that I was pretty certain Holly had described as one of Maddie's favorites. I picked it up and my fingers tingled. It was hers. Somehow, I just fucking knew. That wasn't even supposed to be one of my powers. But I knew. I petted the soft yarn infinity scarf. No fucking way. What were the chances of finding it? It was like I was on a roll. Good thing after fucking good thing! Fuck yes!

I almost looked up at the sky and said thanks, but I was afraid I'd immediately be engulfed in flames. And then we'd lose the scarf and I wouldn't get to see the smile stretch across Ruby's face.

It took all my self-control to calmly hand over ten bucks and walk the fuck outta that place without major Madden touchdown-style celebrations. Bar and Migs whooped when we got outside. Bar tucked the scarf into the pocket of his big down coat for me.

When we reached an empty street I said, "Fuck yeah! Look at us! Good boyfriends!" And I'd never admit it to the guys, but that word boyfriend was a word I'd never used before. And it lit me up inside like a damned firecracker. I was all sparkly-happy and shit.

When we passed Vee, the local nightclub, one of the brawny bartenders was shooing a puppy out the door. The small, white and gold little aussiedoodle whined as Finn, a vamp, nodded to us and used his foot to block the pup from scrambling back through the door. He pulled up the hood of his black hoodie as the sun started to peek over the buildings.

He growled down at the dog. "I said no, mutt! I don't know how you got in here, but you can't stay. Unsanitary hairy bastard."

Bar, the softie, immediately charged forward and scooped up the little dog. "Finn, you got an empty crate or something? I'll take this little guy off your hands."

The bartender grumbled.

Migs wasn't much better. "Dude, that thing could have fleas."

"Girls love puppies," Bar protested.

I crossed my arms over my chest. Ruby was not a normal girl. In a fucking good way. "Did you forget our girlfriend owns a shoe store? What the fuck do puppies love to chew more than bones? Shoes!"

Bar pouted. "Fine. He won't be for Ruby. We'll give him to Holly." He bent down and ruffled the pup's ears. "Right, Dumbledore? You'll be a good boy for Holly."

Migs shook his head as Finn tossed a crate at Bar, who turned and let the crate hit his side as he bodily protected the puppy.

Migs walked over and picked up the crate, setting it upright and holding it while Bar placed the little dog gently inside. "Bar, you can't name the dog you're gonna give to someone else."

Bar shrugged as he picked up the crate and got a faceful of yippy, jumping puppy nips. Then he carried it as we made our way over to Jewels Cafe. He waited outside while Migs grabbed coffee and I ran around town trying to hit quotas before I spent the entire day with my crew again. I knew my boss was pissed, so I at least had to do the minimum.

Everything was going so good for me, that I had to do whatever I could to hold off the bad.

But when I walked back around the corner twenty minutes later, everything that could have gone wrong had.

Ruby was on the sidewalk, dressed in a form-fitting white sweater dress, white tights and little furry booties. Holly stood next to her in a VSCO girl outfit, an oversized hoodie and seashell necklace. John—back in his choir robes—was next to the girls on the sidewalk facing Migs and Bar. For some reason, it looked like they were facing off.

The puppy ran amok, darting around Bar's feet, purple yarn trailing from his mouth.

Shit.

I ran forward. But the red-veined rage in John's face and the white cast of Ruby's cheeks said it all.

Something bad had happened.

We were fucked.

CHAPTER 13

Ruby

"I told you this morning they were sabotaging your miracle!" John thundered next to me, pointing an accusing finger at Bar and Miguel. "Here's the proof! They sent me off with wild accusations of angelic abuse. But those weren't even angels! Those were humans playing dress up! And now, look. Last night they took you to the wrong shop. This morning, they went to the right shop and destroyed the only bit of Maddie's clothing they could find!" John pointed at the bit of purple yarn trailing across the sidewalk from the mouth of a tiny white and gold puppy.

His yelling caused the little dog to yip and hide behind Bar's legs. It caused a few people at the bakery across the street to come outside and stare at us. I could tell it wasn't an admiring kind of stare.

Bar scooped up the dog and cuddled it, saying, "It was an accident. Dumbledore just got carried away."

"More lies!" John thundered. "The demon must have told you we needed clothing for a séance. And you deliberately destroyed it!"

I swallowed hard, insecurity bubbling up in my stomach as my eyes flitted from Migs to Bar. "Is that true?" Even asking that felt like I was cutting myself open. Did demons know about séances? *Did Parker tell them to do this?* I wondered.

Migs shook his head. "No. Ruby. You know we wouldn't. We didn't know anything about that. We just know what you said. You wanted to find Maddie's stuff for Holly. That's it." Migs stuffed his hands into the pockets of his leather jacket as the wind blew harder. But *Harmony's Guide* said liars hid their hands. Was he cold? Or was he lying?

Parker ran up to stand beside the guys, looking heartbreakingly handsome with his wind-tossed hair and grey suit.

But my brother pointed an accusing finger at him and said, "This one! This demon! I bet you he's working on a promotion! Wants to look good, dragging an angel down to the depths. He heard you had two strikes and thought, 'Easy pickings.'"

"Wait, demons are real?" Holly asked.

John had accidentally sprung the whole angel thing on her this morning, when she'd come into the store and he'd materialized out of thin air. At first, she'd screamed and thrown things at him, nearly ruining a beautiful pair of cauliflower-colored slides. But then she'd listened. And I think she believed. Or wanted to anyway. Because she wanted heaven for her sister.

Holly had been devastated to learn Maddie was a ghost.

Holly's eyes were wide with fear when I turned from the argument to look at her.

"There are demons?" she repeated.

I nodded and grabbed her hand to reassure her. "Yes. But Parker's only a minor tech demon—"

"So he says!" John barked. "But demons lie!"

A human with long blonde hair stepped out of Jewels Cafe. He wore an apron, so I assumed he worked there. He walked over to us and said, "Can you take this somewhere else? You're scaring off all our customers!"

John held up his hands, indicating he meant no harm. "We'll leave."

The cafe owner nodded and went back inside.

My brother put an arm around my shoulders and started to bodily turn me.

I resisted, dropping Holly's hand, stepping away from

John, and studying the faces of the men I'd thought were my soulmates. Bar looked devastated, his dark brown eyes wide and brow furrowed. Migs looked shocked, or maybe lost, like he couldn't quite understand. Part of me wanted to go to him and hold his hand like he'd done for me yesterday. But the other part of me doubted, felt insecure. I had a bit of Mig's soul. So I was connected to them. But so did Parker. And he'd been there first.

Was he more evil than I'd recognized? Was I that bad of an angel? Was I that gullible?

I'd been dancing this morning, after the fun we'd had last night. It had been like war only without the real fear. Without the consequences. I'd been happy dancing so hard I hadn't even complained when I stubbed my toe. That's how magnificent it had felt to think I had soulmates.

But staring at the dark expression that came over Parker's face after John's accusation was like staring at that shit demon that had nearly smothered me in 93-93-91, the number planet. I felt like I couldn't breathe. Like the air was putrid and foul and tainted. That day, with the shit demon trying to fill my mouth, I'd felt sure I was going to be given a Science Award for my death—awards for those angels who died the most embarrassingly awful deaths. Today, I felt like I might end up being the first angel to receive that award without dying. "Here is Ruby. The idiot who was foolish enough to fall for a soulmate trick from two humans and a demon, even though she knew humans don't believe in love. Even though she knew one of the guys *was* a demon. Don't be like Ruby." I'd be a nighttime story for little angels as they were put to bed, a warning about everything not to do. Anger rushed through me like lava and I felt so glad that I hadn't mated with them last night. So glad my humiliation wasn't complete in every way.

I glared at the guys and said, "Just go!"

Bar hid his face in the dog's fur.

Mig's took a step toward me. "Corazón, you can't be serious. We'd never—"

Parker stopped him. "It's better if we do what she wants."

My temper flared. He wasn't even going to deny it? He wasn't even going to argue?

Migs and I took a step forward at the same time, our mouths running wild.

"Cerra el orto pelotudo de mierda," Miguel spat at Parker.

At the same time, I said, "You aren't even going to fight? You're not gonna defend yourself?"

Parker said softly, "There's no defending what I am."

There was silence for a moment.

John tugged on my shoulder again.

"You guys are cocksuckers, you know that?" Holly flipped them off.

Bar walked forward and pushed the tiny dog into Holly's

hands. "Here. In our attempts to sabotage everything and do evil we got him for you. I named him Dumbledore. But you can pick whatever."

The little furball licked Holly on the face. She bit down on a smile and pulled a little bit of purple yarn out of the dog's mouth.

"It's okay to like the dog," I told her.

She hugged the dog a little closer. "This doesn't make you guys less assholey," she warned.

Bar nodded.

Holly clung to the little piece of yarn and the dog as I put an arm around her and turned away from my soulmates.

I tried to ignore the stupid human emotions that tugged at me, screamed at me, lit themselves on fire.

I didn't have time for emotions.

I had miracles I needed to make happen.

CHAPTER 14

BARRISTER

I WANTED TO DIE.

We went home, silent and somber, as the sun rose higher in the cloudless sky and the day turned warm and chipper. I glared up at the sun as Migs unlocked the door to our place. Stupid ass sun, it should be ashamed to be out today. The shadows of our apartment felt more right. None of us bothered to turn on the lights as we tromped in.

Parker went right to the liquor cabinet.

Migs—being responsible—sat on a kitchen stool and set up a recording for our shop phone saying we were closed today for a family emergency.

Family emergency, more like implosion.

I marched past both those fuckers to the bathroom. I yanked off my stupid, over-sized coat with the stupid under-sized pockets that had let that stupid dog ruin every damned thing about my life.

I yanked open the medicine cabinet on the back of the mirror.

I took three fucking Benadryl to knock me out and slurped them down with water.

I abandoned my coat on the bathroom floor and shuffled down the hall to my bedroom, trying not to think at all. I just needed to pretend yesterday never existed.

If I forgot yesterday, forgot her, then everything would be alright.

If I forgot the most perfect woman who'd ever existed, the most beautiful, sweet, innocent … If I forgot …

I locked my door and collapsed on my bed, ignoring Migs and Parkers' requests to talk.

I didn't want to talk.

I didn't want to feel.

I didn't want to exist.

Thank ~~God~~ someone for fucking Benadryl because I p … a…s…s…e…d… o…u…t.

CHAPTER 15

RUBY

FIVE HOURS INTO OUR SÉANCE, A SÉANCE ATTEMPTED WITH a tiny piece of purple yarn on the floor of the backroom of my shop, we hadn't seen Maddie once. Not so much as a semi-transparent nipple. I stood and rubbed my aching back, trying to walk out the stiffness in my joints. I tripped and nearly faceplanted on the rough concrete. We'd left the lights off since we'd been trying to summon midday. And I'd thought the light from the high, narrow windows in my backroom was more than enough for simple walking. Apparently not.

For a second, I wished that Parker was here to catch me. Until I remembered he was a lying asshole of a demon who'd convinced two humans to trick me.

"Should have had that stupid boob reduction," I muttered

ANN DENTON

as I paced back and forth through the stock room. Because apparently, without them here, my balance problems were back.

"What was that?" my brother asked.

"Nothing." I waved him off. I didn't need him going on any further. He'd lectured me enough on the walk back here.

What I needed to do was focus. I could walk right down to the graveyard and see the ghosts no problem. But Holly was human. She could see supernaturals now that she knew about the supe world. But ghosts? Human eyes still couldn't detect them without a séance.

And ours wasn't working.

At first, Holly had laughed at me. John had chuckled.

Because I was a screw up and everybody knew it. Last year, I'd tried to reunite a man with his ex-wife only to walk in on her marriage to someone else. That's how much I sucked at miracle-making. At understanding love.

The faces of the guys popped into my head and I tried to shove them away. But stupid tears came anyway.

I swiped them away before Holly noticed. I smiled as she took the little dog outside for a potty break.

As soon as she left, it felt like I could drop the facade of hope and cheer. I turned desperately to John. "Why isn't it working?"

He shook his head. "I'm not sure."

"We've followed your manual exactly," I pointed to the scroll that unfurled across the floor. Next to it was a cross. Three candles flickered dumbly in the light of midday. It was noon. And nothing was working. "I can't mess this up, John. It's my last shot," I rasped as tears clogged my throat.

"I know that!" John said, worrying his lower lip with his teeth. "I'm gonna run upstairs real quick to check—"

"No!" I cried.

But it was too late. My brother shrank into a ball of light and popped out of existence.

Holly came back just as I was gathering up John's robe.

"What the hell happened?" she looked at the clothes in my hands.

"John ran to heaven to check on the protocol." I swallowed hard.

Admitting my incompetence was hard. Watching Holly's face distort as she registered what I was saying was even harder.

Her expression went from disbelieving to harsh. "You mean you haven't done this before?" She gave a laugh. But not a funny one. She squeezed her dog until it yipped, and then she let it down. It ran off through the shelves, eager to get away from her anger.

"This is pointless!" Holly shook her head. She sat back down on one of the folding chairs we'd dragged over to our circle. She leaned forward, hugging her arms to herself. "We're just wasting our time."

Alarm pierced me. "Please ... don't say that."

Holly started to cry softly. "I'm never gonna see her again. She's gone and this is pointless." Her mascara turned her tears into black little raindrops that stained her skin like sin stains a soul. Her aura darkened. "This whole fucking thing is so fucked up. Life is pointless."

I wanted to approach her. I wanted to hug her. But I didn't. Because she was angry. And if I'd learned anything from my own human body, it was that anger demanded space. It deserved to be respected. Because it came from a place of truth. Even if it was wrong. Truth and right weren't always the same thing. But I realized they both deserved respect. Holly's truth was fury.

Hell, it was my truth, wasn't it? I was furious with Parker and Bar and Migs. And I didn't need a hug so I could tamp down on my anger and pretend everything was okay, pretend it didn't exist. I hurt. I felt like a fool for letting them trick me.

I wondered if Holly thought the same of me. Fear set in and I leaned forward. "I want you to know, I am trying my hardest. I'm so sorry you got a defective angel. I wish you hadn't. You deserve a better angel."

And she did. If God had sent someone else, this would

have been so much easier. So much better. I couldn't help but kick myself for agreeing to Maddie's request. I should have sent it off to Gunther and let him assign someone else. I should have stopped the first day—

Holly's words interrupted me as she stood and shoved aside her chair. "A better angel? I don't even know if there's a God. If there was, *He* wouldn't let shit go down like this. There wouldn't be bullshit accidents, choking on grapes. Guys wouldn't be assholes." She kicked over a shoe box.

I bit my lip but didn't say anything.

She grabbed a clothing rack, with outfits we used to dress our mannequins. She yanked a dress off of it. She hurled it aside, but being mostly silk, it wasn't quite the projectile she'd intended. The yellow skirt billowed out like a sail and the entire thing rippled gracefully before falling gently to the ground. Holly stared at it. I stared at Holly.

She was breathing hard. Her hands grabbed at her sweater and she wrapped her arms around herself defensively. Her blue eyes met mine.

"Aren't you going to argue?"

I shook my head. "You're allowed to have your opinion."

"But you disagree. I can see it all over your face."

"What's all over my face?" I reached up and touched my cheek. I didn't feel anything. Was there chalk from the spirit slate I'd written Maddie's name on at the start of the séance?

"Don't be an asshole. Argue with me. You're an angel, right? Tell me why I'm wrong. Why the fuck is this worth it?" Holly threw her arms up.

I shrugged. "You get to decide if it is." Under my breath I added, "Isn't that, right there, enough?"

"What did you say?" Holly marched toward me, her eyes blazing. "You muttering about me?"

I shook my head, and my throat tightened. Bitterness colored my tone when I said, "You have no idea how much I wish I was you." *Able to love and choose. Even if you wanted to choose a lying demon and his friends, you could.*

"What?" That stopped her short. "Don't fucking mock me!" She swiped a sleeve across her snot-filled nose. I didn't bother to tell her that it left a little snail trail behind.

I took a step forward as I saw more tears start to track down her cheeks. I didn't mean to, but in my anger, a little bit of Heaven's light escaped from my palms and lit me from below. "You *get* to decide. You *get* to choose Him. Or reject Him. You get to decide if you believe in a point or not. *You*. It's all about you. What *you* want. Your existence is whatever you want it to be."

Holly gave a broken laugh. "That's such a crock of shit."

Sometimes humans were so arrogant. I gave a single

shoulder shrug as I pursed my lips. "You wouldn't think so if you were in my shoes. Eternal existence. Assignment after assignment. No choice. No freedom. If I make a mistake—guess where I go? Hell. Yeah. This, right here, I'm looking at my last mistake. If you fuck up, you can apologize two seconds before you croak and *whoosh*, elevator service to the top floor!"

Holly swiped at her face again then tossed her middle finger up in the air. "Fuck you. That's not true! That's what you want people to think so they'll bow down and do whatever you say."

That hit a nerve. That right there. "Right. I'm into lying. I'm a fucking angel! I can't lie even when I want to! I can't fall in love even when I want to!" The guys faces flickered in my head.

"Yeah, well some people don't get the chance to do that shit either. Because you let them die."

That made no sense. I stopped short.

"What?"

"Maddie never fell in love. She never got to do what she wanted. She didn't get to 'decide!'" Holly's air quotes were more like jabs. "She didn't get to have a purpose or anything."

I took a long moment to stare at Holly. And I saw her pain, raw and bleeding. My eyes filled with tears. Maybe I was a fuck up as an angel. But her sister had to know that Maddie was special. I cleared my throat, because even thinking about how good Maddie had been to me made me want to cry. Then I said, "Your sister might have died early, but that doesn't make her existence meaningless. She was the first fucking being on this planet to befriend me. Actually befriend me and not just want some miracle out of me like those jerkwads I met at the retirement home with George.

"Maddie taught me things. All kinds of random things, like how to dress and how to order shoes. She came up with the idea for this shop because she knew you liked shoes and I was obsessed with them. And she thought we needed to meet." I had to pause to brush away tears. "I only know English as well as I do because of her. If she hadn't been there," I shook my head. "You might think her existence was wasted. But for me, it was heaven-sent."

A strange blue light flickered next to Holly. And with a pop, Maddie materialized.

"Holy fuck!" Holly shouted, leaping backward.

Maddie turned to look at her sister. The diamond in her nose sparkled, and with the power of the seance, she had a tiny hint of color to her transparent form. I could see the streaks of rainbow in her hair. I could see the punk rock, throwback nature of her outfit.

"Holly?" Maddie asked.

Holly collapsed into tears and Maddie floated over to her. She knelt beside her sister as the little golden dog came running toward his mistress, dragging a high heel in his mouth.

The pup stumbled into Holly's lap and she crushed him to her chest as she stared up at Maddie.

I took a step back, toward the door. "I'll just give you a minute."

Maddie looked over at me and mouthed, "Thank you."

I nodded, my heart full of happiness and aching sorrow at the same time.

I'd gotten Holly to believe. She'd get to say goodbye to her sister. Hopefully this meant things would take a turn for the better.

My miracle would be fulfilled.

I'd get to stay an angel.

That thought should have made me happy. I should have been flying around the room full of excitement.

But I wasn't.

I couldn't share this moment with my soulmates. Tricked, lied to or, whatever I might have been—a victory I didn't share with them felt hollow.

I WAS SITTING IN THE FRONT ROOM OF MY SHOP, IGNORING potential customers who saw me inside but couldn't open the front door. I didn't feel in the mood for selling shoes. I felt like curling up on my furry rug for a good cry.

A ball of light appeared at my feet and shot up toward the ceiling of my showroom like a comet in reverse. It bounced off the ceiling and slowed until it came to hover near face height.

Gunther's voice came out of the ball. "Well, then. That was unexpected, Ruby."

I held up my hand to block the brightness. "What?"

"You completed your Christmas miracle nearly a month early and got a ghost to cross to the good side."

"She crossed?"

"Apparently, she wanted to make sure her sister was alright first. But yes, she crossed. You completed your miracle."

I gave an unenthusiastic shrug. "Yup."

Gunther sputtered. "Shouldn't you be happier? I mean, Ruby, your miracle worked out, thank goodness. But you've done the unheard of."

I stood. "What?" A little shiver went through me. Had I still messed something up? Was something still wrong? It was the soul inside me, wasn't it? I cringed at the thought of having to give it back. "I didn't mean to do something bad."

"Bad! No! Insane maybe. Ruby, you got a demon to offer to give up a bit of soul and get a mark in the good book."

I staggered backward, tripped over one of those metal foot-measuring devices and fell right onto my fuzzy rug. My heart beat frantically. I didn't even care about my sore ass. "Are you sure? When did that happen?"

"Of course, I'm sure. News came directly from Him. Last night, Parker offered to give up his bit of soul so Bar could be with you."

My hands flew to my cheeks. For some reason, that made me happier and more scared than the first day I tried my wings. "What happened?"

"Bar said no. He said that offering to give you up meant Parker deserved you."

My hand flew to my heart, which got as warm and gooey as a fresh chocolate chip cookie. "What about this morning?" My voice was soft, hesitant.

Gunther bobbed up and down as though his light was nodding at me. "They were just trying to help. Accidents happen."

Black holes! Fucking black holes and asteroids! Lightning bolts and black asteroid holes! I'd been in an earthquake once, on planet Ploop. I hadn't been as shaken then as I was now. I was wrong. *My poor sweet men! I was wrong about them! And so was my brother! My perfect brother? Wrong? That can't be right.*

ANN DENTON

I turned to Gunther. "John was wrong?"

John popped into the room just then. A woman outside the window screamed, because John had left his robe here last time he disappeared and hadn't bothered to grab a new one from his cloud on his way back down. I turned to look at John. I couldn't tell, because Gunther was a ball of light, but it looked like he did the same.

"Wrong—" John said, sitting down on one of my white chairs despite his nudity. "Just came in on the last bit of that conversation. Yup. I checked the latest scrolls upstairs. Read that your heart has to be clear and inviting to summon a ghost. You have to fully focus on the person you want to appear. So, you just needa' forget those guys—"

"Wrong," I said. "I need to do the opposite."

"Actually, John," Gunther spoke up, his ball turning spiky and orange. "In spite of your mentorship, your sister seems to have succeeded. Which, in turn, I'm sure, will help when you request this whole female tentacle debacle be put behind you."

The wind was knocked out of me. I turned to John, my mouth agape.

His cheeks grew red.

"Tentacle debacle?" I asked. "That was you?"

John ran a sheepish hand over his neck.

My perfect brother had messed up? I couldn't help it. I

laughed. "Oh, we're two of a kind. I always thought I was the black sheep."

John shrugged. "Guess not. We all have our moments."

Gunther interrupted. "Sorry, but I'm running late for my next meeting because this was unexpected. Well done, Ruby. I'm sorry a choir can't be here to serenade your miraculous success right now; there's a harp tradeshow going on in the Andromeda galaxy." A little slip of parchment shot out of his ball of light and floated down into my hand. "But here's your raincheck for a song. Also, the Wing Council has determined that you can go back to heaven and have your full-size wings restored."

My hands reached back to touch my small, undersized wings. For the past year, I'd hated them. But … Parker had called them dainty yesterday. Migs had stroked them until I'd nearly exploded with pleasure. Bar had had a fit last night during a soda break between video game campaigns when I'd told him that normally my wings covered my ass. Remembering his sputtering, red-faced protests that nothing should cover my ass made me smile.

When I'd decided on this miracle, I'd been determined to get my big wings back. I glanced at my reflection in the full-length mirror that customers normally used to check their shoes. But I'd had my small wings when I met my guys. My wings might not help me fly. They might not be perfect, but they'd become part of who I was down here. Just like my soul. And my soulmates. My chest tightened painfully at that thought. I shoved it away and tried to keep emotion out of my voice as I

ANN DENTON

turned to squint at Gunther's shining light. "No. I'm good. Thanks."

Gunther's light turned orange and then bright blue. I had no idea why. Maybe I'd surprised him. "John, you've been assigned back to your normal post."

John gave a nod and waved at me, before he turned into a ball of light and popped out of existence, the only proof he'd ever been here was the butt print on my white chair.

Once he was gone, I turned back to my boss.

I smiled weakly at Gunther's light, which had turned a sparkly red. Thinking about the guys had made my insides mushy, in good ways and bad. I wanted Gunther to leave so I could curl up on my white rug and have a good cry. And then, on the other hand, I didn't want to be alone.

Gunther drifted through the air silently for a minute. And then he said what I least expected. "Ruby, I know last year's miracle made you a little skeptical about love. But it does exist."

"What?"

Gunther's voice was soft as he said, "Love is a miracle. And miracles aren't easy or natural—you know that. Miracles take work." Gunther swirled a soft pink into his red light. "Miracles are also a gift from Him. So accept the gift." He reshaped himself into a heart as he boomed out like an army general, "You know what to do, soldier. Attack. Conquer. Kiss."

I took a step and nearly tripped, but Gunther turned corporeal at the last moment. He caught me. He hugged me against his portly human body and then released me so I could look at him. In human form, Gunther was a hefty man with no hair on his head but huge sideburns, big blue eyes, and a wide smiling mouth. "I'm so happy for you Ruby. So happy. All I've ever wanted was for you to find your place. Find where you fit. And you do fit with them. Perfectly."

I giggled and swiped at my eyes, which seriously teared up far too often. Stupid human waterworks. "That's just like my store sign. The Perfect Fit."

Gunther's cheeks crinkled near his eyes as he smiled down at me fondly. "I know. *He's* really into signs. Kind of one of His quirks."

My heart felt like a cup left under the tap too long. I had looked away for just a second and there it was, overflowing. I finally felt like I knew what it was like to be human. Fully human. To have ridiculous expectations and false hopes and disappointments and false beliefs but to know that, despite all of that surface turmoil, deep down underneath, I was loved. My men loved me. Enough to let me turn around and leave them. Enough to hopefully forgive me when I came charging back.

Because if I'd learned anything from my miracle with Holly, it was that love required forgiveness.

She'd had to forgive Him. I needed them to forgive me.

But that didn't mean I didn't have to earn it.

Gunther left, turning back into a ball of light and disappearing. Unlike John, Gunther took his robe with him.

I went to the back to check on Holly.

She sat on the ground cuddling her new pup, tears still rolling down her face. When she saw me, she rose. Holly wiped her face on her sweater sleeve and came over to give me a giant bear hug. "Thank you," she whispered.

"Of course," I said.

After we'd hugged for what felt like a really long time and my sweater dress had gotten damp, I asked, "Um … so I helped you. And miracles don't require any kind of reciprocity. But I could really use some help."

Holly leaned back and studied my face. "With what?"

"The guys. My boss just said they weren't undermining the miracle. It was all a misunderstanding."

"Shit!"

"Yes. What do humans normally do when they've messed up with their soulmates?"

"Um … like regular people buy flowers and stuff. But regular people don't go around accusing other people of being in league with demons."

I nodded. Right. I was worse. Typical for me and my mistakes. So, I needed to do something bigger. That made sense. "Do you have any examples?"

"Only like in movies, where they like stop a plane from taking off, or there's one where this guy builds a house for the woman he loves, or like writing a song and singing it in public, some kind of big gesture. Like kinda crazy stuff usually. I dunno. I mean, what do they like?"

Inspiration came at me like a bullet. Fast and furious and perfect. I turned to Holly. "Can you go drop that dog off at home and then help me?"

She shrugged. "Sure. What are we doing?"

"I'll tell you as we walk. We're gonna have to move fast."

Holly scooped up her little pup in a snuggle and then I locked up The Perfect Fit. As we walked back to her house, I laid out my plan for redemption.

CHAPTER 16

MIGS

PARKER WAS DRUNK, THOUGH DEMONS COULD BURN IT OFF faster than humans. Bar was passed out in his room. I went to my bedroom and fell onto my plaid comforter, trying not to smile or cry at the fact that Ruby would probably want to burn it. My chest ached in a way it never had before. I'd never dated much, because no one had ever called to me. No soul had sung to mine. Until hers.

And unlike the other two, who were drowning their sorrows, I guess my mind wouldn't let me admit that everything was over. I mean, Ruby was an angel. She'd made a mistake, yes, but she'd come back to us. I believed that. I didn't know why or how. But she had part of my soul. We were connected. And she wouldn't abandon that connection or us. She'd come back. I just had to wait.

I hoped. Doubt started to creep in. I couldn't fight it off alone, so I had to do something desperate to combat it.

I called my mother, trying to distract myself with the chaos of home.

"Ai. Miguelito! Hola. Oh, your auntie just got in. One minute, mijo."

I heard the rustle of clothing as they hugged. My Aunt Lucia was always coming over. She was a great distraction though. Because she was a widow and a gossip. She knew everyone at home. If I could get her on the line, I could fill my ears with hours of random tidbits about everyone. Hopefully that would keep the doubt at bay and be long enough for Ruby to come to her senses.

I heard Lucia and my mother start to chatter like birds and I said, "Hello! Hello! I'm still here!"

My mother didn't pick back up the phone. My aunt must have swiped it from her. "Miguel! How are you? Have you met anyone nice? Any good Argentenian girls moved to that town of yours yet?"

I shoved aside the thought of Ruby. Picturing her pouty lips was painful. And while I needed to hold onto hope, I couldn't jinx it by talking about her. Ugh. Just that stupid superstitious thought had me mad at myself. It wasn't even logical. But then, what really was? It felt so hard to balance what I'd always thought of as true and what was true now that I knew Ruby. I rested an arm behind my head as I lay back on the bed. "Tia Lucia. Hola. Just working. Like always."

"I had a dream of you the other night, you know? Did your mama tell you?—Elena, you didn't tell him! Why didn't you tell him?!"

I heard the two of them start to bicker. If I let them get going, they'd never stop. "Lucia, Lucia!" I had to shout to be heard.

"Oh, Miguel. Yes. Sorry. What was I saying?"

I snorted, imagining my aunt and my mom. They'd wander into the bright tiled kitchen and my aunt would rearrange everything as she chatted on the phone, my mother following right behind to return things to their rightful place. Lucia was such a character. "You were going to tell me about your dream."

"Oh, yes. My dream. I dreamt you were in the dark. And a woman surrounded by purple sparkles led you out of darkness."

I sighed and rolled onto my side. "If only it were that easy—"

Bang.

I shot up on the bed, dropping the phone.

Bang. Bang.

I ran out of my room, into the hallway. Someone was at the front door, pounding hard.

Parker just stared at me glassy eyed from his spot in his armchair, a tumbler of bourbon in his hand. He followed me down the hall.

I unlocked the door and pulled it open, heart pounding, hoping—

It wasn't Ruby.

"Amethyst?" Parker sounded surprised.

Ruby's best friend raised her hand and said, "Come with me, now. All of you." Her hand lit up with magic, and purple sparkles danced in the air in front of her.

Purple sparkles. Purple fucking sparkles?!

"Fuck yeah!" I punched the air. I pushed past Parker, purposely "Come on, motherfucker, it's time to go see Ruby."

"Whaa?"

I didn't answer him, just sprinted to the kitchen and grabbed a key from the drawer. I unlocked Bar's room and burst inside. I yanked him out of bed. Ugh. He smelled. He hadn't even been drinking. What the hell?

"Shower!" I told him.

Parker stumbled into the doorway.

I turned around and jabbed a finger at him too. "Shower and get dressed. I'm leaving in five minutes with or without you. And if I do, Ruby's all mine."

I went back out into the hall, realizing I'd left Amethyst at the door. I jogged over to her. "Sorry. One sec. They need to clean up. Please have a seat, grab water, whatever." I gave a hurried welcoming gesture toward the couch then ran to my own room, leaving her to close the front door behind her.

Hurry. Hurry. That was all my mind could think. Because purple sparkles leading me to the light. There was only one light I wanted.

I yanked off my wrinkled shirt and put something nicer on. A collared shirt. Not plaid.

I heard a squawking sound and picked up my phone from the bed. "Shit! Sorry, Lucia. Can't talk. The woman with purple sparkles just got here."

The shriek that erupted from the other side of the phone was deafening. I hung up before it shattered my eardrums. I buttoned my shirt and checked my hair in the mirror, whistling as I did. My heart was doing cartwheels and karate chops. I felt like fucking *Kung Foo Fighting*. And that's what I whistled.

Damn. Tia Lucia and her dreams. I'd always thought she was as superstitious as abuela.

I was gonna have to listen to her more often.

CHAPTER 17

Ruby

Night fell early, and that was partially a good thing, partially a bad thing, because Holly and I had to sprint to the gates of Silver Springs Cemetery with bags in our hands to make it before sunset. Good thing we were both wearing The Perfect Fit's latest acquisition—pink Outdoor Voices. Holly had insisted we dress our best for "Project Redemption."

Holly had coordinated her leggings and over-sized sweatshirt to match. I kind of thought she resembled a giant pink tampon applicator, but when I mentioned that, she'd made the grabby choking gesture at my face. So I stopped bringing it up. I wore a white sweater dress. The shoes ruined my flirty look, but that couldn't be helped. Heels were evil. Literally. They were invented by demons in the same division as Parker—the Annoyance and Bad Mood Division. And I wouldn't support them.

Laser guns weren't evil, however. They were fun. And we'd spent nearly forty-five minutes talking to a salesman to make sure we got just the right set.

"This might be the sweetest and lamest thing I've ever heard," Holly said as she reapplied her lip-gloss while we walked up the sidewalk.

"Hush, you're making me more nervous. What if they hate it?" I chewed my lower lip.

She rolled her eyes. "They won't."

I couldn't tell if she was telling the truth or being sarcastic. But at this point, I was out of time to care. We only had minutes. My hands started to shake from nerves. "Just help me get these dumb boxes open before they get here."

She laughed at me when I tried to open the first box. But I excused her because she knew exactly how to unthread all the stupid doohickeys on the back of the laser gun boxes. Why the fuck did the manufacturer's tie their toys up like that? Did they not want anyone to actually use their products? My box ended up a shredded mess of paper and cardboard, like the bottom of a hamster cage.

Holly took the final gun box away from me with a shake of her head. "You're hopeless. Go check everything else inside."

I ran in. Muriel had rounded up twenty-seven ghosts in

all. There were two I hadn't even seen before. "Everyone know the rules?"

Muriel nodded. I sat down and set out my seance candles and pulled out the chalkboard. Muriel flew over and dumped a slew of dirty pebbles in my lap.

"Ugh! What's this?"

"Teeth," she cackled. "You said you needed something from everyone in order to do the seance. That's all most of us have left."

I shuddered, using a candle to roll the teeth to the side. "I didn't mean body parts."

"Picky, picky," Muriel critiqued.

I shoved aside my disgust and did a hurried séance, having each ghost tell me their name one by one. This séance went as smoothly as a cupid's bottom. Each ghost was so cooperative that it was easy to pull them just over the void into visibility. Thank goodness because I was short on time.

I had just finished when a purple flare lit the sky. Shit. Amethyst's signal. The guys were almost here. I abandoned the candles and the ghosts, yelling over my shoulder, "Don't forget the rules!"

Then I booked it to the crypt with the winged horse and tucked a tiny scroll into one of the stone feathers carved on the wing. Then I pulled out the scrap of parchment that Gunther had given me and opened it, saying, "I need a song."

Bright white lights appeared around me, like I was the sun in the middle of some tiny galaxy. It would have been incredibly cool, except it was also incredibly blinding. I squinted and held a hand up between my eyes and the bright light.

"Yes?" a deep baritone boomed.

I cleared my throat. "Yes, hi. Um, Gunther gave me this rain check for a song. Do you happen to know the sound-track for any video games?" I asked hopefully.

One of the lights turned bright purple and said, "Ummm…"

"Like, maybe Resident Evil or something? Something spooky?" I crossed my fingers.

One of the lights snorted and sparked. "Evil! We don't do evil."

I wrung my hands. I didn't have a lot of time to explain. "Okay. Not evil. Just like … scary. Can you do scary?"

One of the lights expanded and popped into an angel, feathers from his wings fluttering to the ground. He scratched his big snub nose as he stared at me. "We can do scary. Remember that Netflix show we just binged, everyone? We'll all have to go corporeal to play instruments."

Groans arose from several balls of light. "Ugh. But human

bodies are so ugly." One of the other lights bonked that light from the side. "Hey!"

I waved my slip of parchment in the air. "Miracle rain check right here. Says I'm entitled to a celestial song. And I know the classical stuff you guys normally sing takes ages so..."

Slowly, each ball of light materialized as an angel wearing a classical white robe and golden belt. All their halos glowed in the dim blue-grey light of dusk. I clenched my fists in excitement so I wouldn't clap like a school girl. Holly was very against clapping. When I had control of myself, I pointed. "Okay, so if you all could hover just over there, above that tree, you are going to be the sound effects."

"Sound effects?" The choir master, the man with the smudge nose who held a baton in his hand, furrowed his brow.

"Just ... fly over there and wait for my signal. Scariest music you can."

The choir master held out his hand and I gave him the rain check. He tucked it into the pocket of his robe and then the angels took up formation above the spooky, leaf-less oak tree, harps and horns and other instruments magically appearing in their hands.

I heard a car horn honk. Shit. Amethyst and the guys were here. I ran, stumbling around headstones, yelling at the ghosts as I passed and waving my arms frantically. "Hide!"

They all obligingly sunk into the ground or crouched behind gravestones. I nearly face planted when I reached the gate and had to flutter my wings furiously to keep myself upright. I wavered for a second, but I managed to regain my balance. Then I yanked open the metal gate, which shrieked in protest, startling Bar as he climbed out of the back of the Uber Amethyst must have rented.

He looked good. Bar was wearing his typical jeans and funny t-shirt combo with just a light jacket. His t-shirt said "Nerd Alert: I'm staring at one." I rolled my eyes, assuming he'd picked it out to wear facing Migs. Bar stopped short at the sight of me.

Migs bumped into him climbing out of the car. "What the —" My Argentinian stood and froze when he saw me.

I gave him an awkward wave. The opposite of Bar, he was wearing a button up shirt and khakis. His hair was perfectly slicked back, while Bar's black curls looked like he might have just showered. Luckily, it had warmed up during the day, otherwise, he'd have been freezing.

My eyes traveled back and forth between the two men. Neither of them spoke. They just stared at me in return.

Parker exited from the other side of the vehicle and walked behind it slowly, his eyes traveling over me from head to toe. He looked so good in his sports coat and white collared shirt. The perfect picture of temptation. But when I met his eyes behind his glasses, I couldn't tell what his gaze meant. I didn't feel the heat from before, the attraction. Was he mad? Furious? Already rejecting me?

My stomach twisted and my throat dried out. "Hi. Um." I gave a weak wave, not sure what to do.

Amethyst didn't even climb out of the car. She just gave me a thumbs up from the front passenger seat and then had the driver pull away.

All three guys watched the car leave.

"I ..." My mind forgot how to English.

Holly strode up the sidewalk, from where she'd been waiting with the bag of laser guns. "Honestly, Ruby. You're hopeless." She pulled a leaf out of my hair and kissed my cheek. Then she turned to those guys. "Ruby has a gift for you. And if you fuckwads don't love it, then you're the stupidest pieces of shit on the planet."

Parker laughed. "I take it the miracle went off alright?"

I nodded.

"Even though we messed it up?" Bar's voice was soft.

I looked over at him. His fingers fidgeted with the seam of his pants, like he was nervous. My feet carried me over to him. Once I was within three feet, my entire body lit up from within. Like it knew I needed to be with him. With them. I leaned forward until Bar was forced to meet my eyes. I looked into the soft warmth of his brown gaze and said. "You didn't mess up. I did."

His eyes started to get shiny—

"Oh, fuck no. You are not doing it this way and screwing

up your whole plan," Holly interjected. She grabbed my hand and yanked me away from the guys, back down the sidewalk with her so she could scoop up the laser guns. She roughly thrust two at me and then marched me back to the guys.

"Alright, dimwits. This is a laser gun." She tossed one to Parker, who caught it. "In there, Ruby's made you your very own video game come to life."

Miguel's jaw dropped.

I was too nervous to move. My hands just locked up on the final laser gun as my eyes flitted from face to face. The guys were exchanging looks with one another. It felt like I was balancing on a rope over a cliff. Until Parker smiled.

Immediately, I realized what he was thinking. I didn't know how I knew it; I just did. Maybe because he was mine—because our souls were connected, because somehow, I knew him, though I couldn't fully explain how. "No cheating, Parker. You are not allowed to sabotage their guns."

He blew a raspberry at me.

Migs punched his arm. "That's right, cabrón. Back off. Or the angel will punish you."

"I might like that," Parker winked at me and my body started to tremble. My nipples tightened at the thought. *Does Parker find timeouts and lectures sexually exciting?* I wondered. I'd do whatever it took to make him happy.

But punishment didn't seem all that thrilling as a mating ritual to me. We'd discuss that later. Hopefully.

"No cheating," I wagged a finger at him.

He walked up to me until he towered over me and his dark eyes burned down into mine. "I'll try. But it's gonna be really hard for me. Do I get a reward if I'm a good boy?" He reached for me.

"Okay, gross. None of that." Holly pulled me back away from him.

Holly grabbed another gun from me and tossed it at Migs.

He fumbled to catch it. "Is this really happening?"

Holly nodded. "Your objective is to get past the ghosts and find the scroll."

A half-smile lit up Bar's face. "Are you serious right now?"

I gave him the final laser gun and our fingers brushed against one another, sending a shiver down my spine. Our eyes locked and I swallowed hard as I nodded.

Holly pushed open the gate, which gave that amazingly awesome ominous creak. It was so perfect for the start of their adventure.

The guys rushed forward, but she held up a hand.

"Ruby?"

I used my wings to flutter past them and stand just inside the iron gate on the grass. I turned and signaled to the

choir master. And the entire choir of angels started up the
theme song from *Stranger Things*. I turned back to see my
guys looking at me. Bar was blinking back tears. I smiled
at him. Then I looked at Migs and the heat from his gaze
started a fire in my loins. Parker's naughty smile told me I
was already forgiven. My heart swelled. It felt so light that
for a second I thought I was flying, even though my feet
were firmly planted on the uneven ground. My vision
misted and I sniffled, about to hug-tackle them.

But then Muriel—always one to ruin a moment—
launched her attack. She screeched, her wrinkled face
elongating and distorting into something horrific as she
flew through the air—her paisley dress streaming out
behind her. Bar screamed, stumbling backward when she
swiped at him. But then, all three guys aimed their lasers.

Muriel got hit with two shots to the chest and one dead-
on headshot. But she didn't stop. She swooped right
through Bar, making him shiver and shriek again.

"Muriel, you're out!" I scolded. "No cheating! They got
you fair and square."

Muriel crossed her arms and pouted, floating just beside
the guys. "That's only because those pigeon-livered
ratbags were supposed to come with me. We were
supposed to do a group attack. I want a redo."

"No!" I told her. "Those aren't the rules!"

But Parker held up a hand. He smiled at the disgruntled
old ghost. "Why don't you go set up near the crypt,

Muriel? It'll give you more time to plan your sneaking and you can be the finale."

Muriel disappeared with a pop and Parker gave me a wink that made my knees weak.

Then Migs took charge. "Okay. We're gonna take it like the game *Left for Dead*. I'll run point. Parker is clean up. Bar, guard flanks and help us—"

The ghosts didn't give them time to finish planning. A man in a top hat flew out of the grass at them. My guys all dived different directions, shooting as they did.

"Fuck!" Migs said as he hit the ground and rolled. "My shoulder!"

"Embrace the pain," Parker said, squatting behind a gravestone and pretending that the scoping mechanism on the laser gun actually worked.

A woman in bell bottoms named Gloria zoomed through three gravestones and latched onto Parker's abdomen. "I'm hit! I'm hit!" he screeched, falling to the ground and writhing like he was in pain.

My eyebrows shot up as the ghost zoomed off. I hurried over to Parker and crouched down beside him. "Are you really hurt?" My eyes scanned his face and started lifting his shirt. His abs looked fine. Well, more than fine. Tempting really. Had she hurt him internally? The ghosts had promised not to go poltergeist. I turned back to look at Parker again.

But he just leaned up and pressed his mouth to mine. His lips were warm and soft. And though it was dark and cold outside, it felt like the sun was rising in my chest. My lips parted and Parker deepened the kiss, his hand coming up to cup my face as his tongue stroked mine.

Migs pulled me backward out of Parker's reach. He was gentle, but his arm wrapped around me in a way that let me know I wasn't allowed to go back to kissing. "What are you doing, man?" he asked Parker as I snuggled into his warm arms.

"Powering up," Parker grinned.

Migs shook his head and pointed his gun at Parker's head. "No. We'll never reach our objective if she's the power up. We have to change it. You have to ... um ..." his eyes searched the graveyard.

Holly jumped in with a suggestion. "You have to run to me and do fifteen pushups."

Bar fist pumped as Migs and Parker groaned.

Another ghost had them all diving behind gravestones, yelling directions at one another and taking the game seriously. It was so fucking cute to see them slip on the same dark, determined faces they wore as they played video games. I slipped over next to Holly and watched them for the next twenty minutes as they got progressively better.

Holly shook her head as she watched them. "I seriously can't believe you won't let me film this. We could put an ad in front of this shit and make millions on YouTube. They are cray-cray."

I shook my head as I gazed fondly at them. Bar attempted a barrel roll but accidentally bumped his head on a gravestone. Migs hit his funny bone leaning around a corner. And Parker couldn't help himself. He kept fucking with any electronics within reach. The lights that lined the gate flickered. Bar's gun went out and he smacked Parker with it.

"I can't help it man. Sometimes when I get excited—" Parker protested.

"You blow your wad early? Focus dude," Bar chastised.

Holly laughed at that.

I just pressed a hand to my heart. Even sniping at each other, my guys were adorable.

Eventually, Holly held up her phone, the video function open. "I wouldn't," I warned her. "Parker will just zap your phone," I told her.

She rolled her eyes. "How can you stand such dorks?"

"Dorks? They're the best. And they helped find your sister's scarf, got you a puppy…"

Holly brushed back her long, blonde hair. "Still dorks."

I rolled my eyes.

"But, like … you're with all three of them," she added softly. "Three *hot* dorks. How did you manage that?"

I shrugged. "Magic."

She shook her head as her phone turned blue and the video she was trying to take died. "Dammit."

"Told you." I shrugged. I had warned her.

She glared at Parker for a second before saying "Well, my work here is done. I don't really want to see any more porno re-enactments, so I'll just be heading home to Snugaboo—"

"Who?"

"The dog."

I patted her shoulder. "Thanks for your help, Holly." I considered giving her a hug, but this was somewhat in public, so I doubted she would let me. I ended up giving her an awkward smile instead. "See you at work tomorrow?"

She nodded. "Enjoy your nerd harem."

I laughed nervously. "I will. I hope. If they forgive me."

Holly shook her head as she tossed her hair up into a quick messy bun. "You really don't get humans at all, lady. You're already forgiven." She winked and walked toward the gate. As it screeched open, I heard her muttering. "I need to get me a fucking magic harem. Fuck."

CHAPTER 18

PARKER

WE MADE IT TO THE CRYPT JUST AS THE SUNSET EVAPORATED and darkness replaced it. I only had to power up three times during our battle to get here. A damned baby ghost kept getting me. Kid was freaky as shit—turning his head in a full circle as he toddled around.

I shivered just thinking about him as the wind picked up and added to the creep factor. I took a step closer to the crypt. It was some Weatherhouser creation. It had their big flying horse logo on the side. My eyes started roaming the grey stone sides, looking for the scroll that Ruby told us to find.

That hag Muriel dive-bombed us. She ignored the laser shots we put right through her as she barreled into me. Damn. She'd make an awesome poltergeist, if I ever recommended her to the Haunting division. Normally, I was all about favors and connections. But today, now, not so much.

Finding the scroll was far more important. So, I pretended Muriel didn't exist, even as she blasted us with icy wind. I just crawled around the base of the crypt as Bar and Migs did the same.

I found a tiny slip of rolled parchment.

"I got it!" I called out and the guys crowded around. I waited until they were ready before I opened it.

It was perfect, just like our Ruby.

> **I'm sorry. I was wrong. I've been told to offer you make up sex. I didn't think guys liked wearing makeup.**
>
> **Alternative suggestion: We could try that mating thing we almost did in the alley. If you're not ready for that though, I'm happy to play more video games to prove my worth as a mate.**

I looked at Bar first. He looked flabbergasted. Migs looked like he was in physical pain. Fucking Ruby. How could a woman be this perfect?

"Who's going first?" he asked.

That was indeed the question. Ruby walked slowly toward us, weaving her way through the gravestones. The demon in me wanted her first, wanted that glory, and that instant gratification. But I couldn't. My shard of soul wouldn't let me.

When Ruby reached us, I said, "All for one?"

Migs immediately nodded as he yanked Ruby toward him and dipped her in a hot kiss. God, watching her back arch like that gave me ideas. The girl was flexible.

Bar still hadn't answered. I turned to look at him. He stared at Migs kissing Ruby a moment longer before he turned to me. He held up a fist. "And one for all."

We bumped, making it official.

And then we carried our sweet angel back home, trading her every block or so. When it was my turn, I put my forehead to hers. The connection between us was so visceral it felt like a net pulling me closer, closing me in. It felt like Ruby was my air. I slid my hand up her back and felt those soft wings. I trailed my fingers over them just like I had the other night.

Her eyes dilated and her breathing grew rapid. I couldn't resist trailing my lips over her pulse as Migs unlocked the door to our place. I handed her off to Bar and let him carry her over the threshold, knowing he was a sucker for that sappy shit.

When we got inside, I locked the door behind us. And then I turned to everyone in the living room and said, "My room."

I had a king bed, where the others only had queens. And

my room was decorated in greys with a naughty crimson comforter that would look amazing with Ruby laying on top of it. I wanted that image of her burned into my mind for the rest of my existence.

I stood by the door, breathing hard as Migs and Bar stood on either side of her and she traded kisses with them. Migs got aggressive first, his leg sliding between her thighs and teaching her how to move to please herself as he kissed her. He lifted her skirt, exposing the gorgeous pale skin under that sweater dress. Skin that looked as soft as silk. I could just see the curve at the bottom of her ass, the lacy edge of her pure white panties. Migs bunched her skirt around her thighs and held Ruby steady as she spread her wings and her lips parted. "Oh!"

My dick twitched. Part of me wanted to take my phone out and take photos of Ruby because she looked so hot it was unbelievable. But a bigger part of me didn't want the chance of anyone else seeing her like this—ever.

Migs gestured for Bar to come up on the side. "Stroke her wings and suck her neck," he ordered.

Just hearing him order around Bar made my blood run hot. Ruby arched back, those perfect tits pointing skyward under that soft sweater dress as Bar's tongue swiped over her neck. It sent a shudder down my spine. I stepped closer.

Miguel's eyes narrowed to slits as he told me, "Gently tease her breasts. I want her wild."

Three of us, at once? I glanced at Ruby for a second, unsure if that would be too much. She was an angel, after all. A virgin.

Ruby's eyes glanced over at me; they were big grey pools of seduction that a man or a demon could drown in. "Aren't you supposed to kiss me too, to start the mating process? Or are you not ready yet?"

Oh, I was ready. I was locked and loaded like a damned missile. Countdown had already started.

I cleared my throat as I came up beside her. "I just don't want to overwhelm you. And my natural instincts aren't to be sweet. So I thought—"

Ruby's hand lifted and swiped gently over my jawline, a smile transforming her perfect face. "I trust you."

I'd fought angels before. Been pierced by their arrows of light and goodness. But this felt like an angelic bomb had exploded in my chest. It felt like sun rays were ripping right through me and dissolving the darker parts of myself. I leaned forward and kissed Ruby, kissed my soulmate.

Her trust—it meant everything. And with my kiss I vowed to do whatever it took to keep that trust.

I deepened our kiss, my tongue plunging into her mouth. I was surprised when she matched my aggression stroke for stroke. But Ruby was full of good surprises. One of her hands came to my neck, and then dragged slowly down my shirt.

I reached forward and gently stroked her breasts through her dress like Migs had commanded. I swiped my fingers along the sides, underneath, along the top. I avoided her nipple until she broke our kiss, panting with need.

"What, what is that?" she asked, nodding her head toward her breasts.

I gave her a naughty wink as I grazed her nipples.

Her body jerked between my touch. "That!"

"Just wait, Ruby. I have a few tricks up my sleeve," I muttered, as Migs hands reached down and squeezed her ass before helping her slide more quickly up and down his thigh.

"Tricks?" Ruby asked. "Like dog tricks?"

We all laughed, and she got this glorious little pout.

Migs soothed it away by leaning forward and nipping at her lip. "No, querida. Dearest, it's a sexual trick."

I tweaked her nipples and said, "You know how I short out all those computers and things? They run on electrical impulses. Just like this hot little body …" And then I sent the tiniest surge of electricity into Ruby's nipples.

"Ahhh," she cried out, writhing against Migs. "Yesss! Whatever that means, do it again."

Migs held up a hand to stop us. "First, we want to see you naked, Corazón."

We all stepped back, like the three of us were in sync, which somehow, surprisingly, we were.

Ruby went to yank up her dress, but Migs shook his head. "Slowly, please."

And then Ruby did the most agonizingly hot strip tease I'd ever seen. She didn't even mean to, she just took Migs at his word. She slowly dragged her dress up inch by inch, until we could see her innocent, lacy white panties. The wet spot on the crotch made my hand fly to my dick and I stroked the length through my suit pants. Fuck.

The dress went up over her head and she let it dangle in her hand for a minute as we took in her breasts. Ruby did not know how to buy the right size bra. Thank fuck for that, because her tits were spilling out of the thing and the tops of her nipples were visible over the lace. My mouth watered. I wanted to latch on and suck for days.

Ruby's hands caressed her stomach, probably because she was cold, but to me it felt like she was torturing us in the best way possible. Because I ached to touch that skin.

"Now the bra," Migs ordered, his Hispanic accent was doubled in the heat of the moment.

I glanced over at him, and at Bar, trying to gauge their reactions to this situation. I knew Bar was the most timid. But when I looked at his face, there was no reservation. He was utterly focused on Ruby as the palm of one of his hands brushed back and forth over the head of his cock through his jeans.

I turned back to see Ruby's breasts revealed for the first time. And they were perfect. Heavy as cantaloupes but her nipples pointing up at an angle enticingly.

Migs started to order her to take the panties, but I held up a hand. "Can Bar and I help her do it?" I asked.

Migs and I both looked at Bar, who just silently walked across the grey carpet to stand on Ruby's right side. I walked over to her left.

Ruby's hands came out to hug both of us to her. And the feel of her skin made instinct take over. I couldn't help it. I leaned forward and took one of those nipples that had been teasing me between my lips. I rolled the soft nub gently between my teeth until it stiffened further, and then I started lapping at it. I felt Bar's arm brush mine and glanced sideways only to see him doing the exact same thing.

Ruby's hand flew to the back of my head and pushed my face closer.

"That feels so good," her voice was breathy.

Tiny gusts of wind swept over us and I realized Ruby was batting her wings in response to our stimulation. Her feet started to lift off the ground. My hand flew to her ass to hold her in place and I found myself touching Bar's hand, because he'd done the same. I expected him to pull away, but he didn't. His fingers just dug into the tender flesh of Ruby's perfect round ass.

Migs voice came from behind Ruby as he said, "I think

you guys forgot what you were supposed to be doing." He smacked our hands away and yanked down Ruby's panties himself.

I had to see.

I let go of her nipple and leaned back, even though her hand tried to press me forward again.

"Parker!" she whined.

I glanced down, over her tiny stomach, to the gorgeous patch of dark curls and the pink petals that looked ready to be devoured.

Two male hands reached between Ruby's thighs and pulled her open. I leaned down more so I could see that perfect pink slit. And I couldn't help it. That inner selfish demon, that beast who needed to claim his mate, roared, and I dived forward, desperate to taste Ruby.

Unfortunately, Bar and I had the exact same idea. At the exact same moment. Our heads collided with a *crack*.

Fucking hell! We both fell back on our asses holding pounding skulls.

"That's what you both get for not listening," Migs chided, as his fingers started to work that gorgeous slit in front of our eyes.

Ruby's body tensed and she said, "This feels just like the alley. Oh, my twinkly stars! Yes! I love it. Keep going Migs. Please. I need you to mate with me."

Migs used one of his fingers to thrust up into Ruby as his other hand circled her clit. As he thrust in and out, I could see how wet he made her. A few orgasms, and her body would be ready for us.

I stood and threw off my clothes.

"What are you doing?" Bar asked, shielding his eyes.

"Dude, I'm planning on making love to our soulmate. If you're just gonna watch, that's fine by me. Otherwise, you might wanna get ready."

Bar made a face but tossed off his shirt, revealing abs I'd admired more than once. "Don't let your dick touch mine," he warned.

I rolled my eyes. "Wasn't planning on it."

He shucked his pants and then we both stood there stroking ourselves as Ruby turned my room into a whirlwind, her little wings flapping as fast as a hummingbird as Migs brought her to her first ever orgasm.

"Holy fucking lightning bolts!" she screamed as her body twisted and convulsed on Migs hands. Her hands reached out for something to latch onto and I was there in an instant. I stroked her wings as she came, trying to draw out the sensation.

Bar went to her other side and dropped to his knees. As she started to come down, he moved aside Miguel's hand. He leaned forward and started lapping at Ruby with his tongue.

I had to think of our video game stats for a minute to keep myself from spurting. I'd always imagined watching Bar eat a girl out. I'd never thought the day would come when I would actually get to see it.

Migs worked his way up Ruby's body and rubbed her back and wings for a second, before stepping back to get undressed himself.

I reached forward and pinched one of Ruby's nipples.

She turned her head and her soft lips just had to be kissed. So, I leaned down and kissed her, listening to her moans and feeling her quiver as Bar used his tongue to get her worked up again. When she was close, I started sending tiny pulses of electricity through my fingers, just enough to make her tits bounce and the sensation shoot through her nervous system.

Ruby pressed into me harder, breaking off our kiss and nuzzling into my neck. "Is this mating?" she asked. "I thought you had to be inside me."

"This is foreplay, baby. We're getting your body ready to mate."

"Foreplay—"

I leaned back down and captured her lips. This time I sent a little electricity from my lips to hers. And damn! The sensation shot down my body as well, lighting my dick up like a fucking Christmas tree. I let go of Ruby's nipple for a second and brought her hand to my dick. I wrapped her tiny fingers around it and reveled in the sensation as I showed her how to stroke me. She did so perfectly, gentle, teasing, edging me as if she knew what the fuck that was.

Her grip got tighter on me as she started to thrash against Bar's face. His hands came up to hold her still and I clamped my own hands down on her waist to hold her in place.

She grew frantic, bucking and wild, throwing one of her legs up over Bar's back as she rode him to completion.

My eyes met Migs. Nothing had ever been so hot. Ever.

When Ruby came down from her high, I had to help her, so she didn't pitch face-first onto my floor. My sweet little soulmate was on the verge of collapse. I carried her over to my bed and set her on top of the mattress. She splayed out, wings and legs wide, completely unaware of how fucking tempting she looked. Her breasts rose and fell as she caught her breath. And my hand had to squeeze the base of my dick, cut off the blood flow, so I wouldn't come just at the sight of her.

When she'd recovered enough to look down at us, she said, "I thought there was more."

Migs crawled up on the bed first. "There is, Corazón. But we want to take it slow for you."

"Oh, you don't have to go slow."

"Trust me, it's better," Migs replied.

"I trust you." Ruby smiled.

"Good," Migs held himself over her in a push up position. He kissed her. His erection poked into her stomach. But he pulled back from the kiss and said, "I think Bar should go first."

I glanced over at the man who'd shared his soul with me. His eyebrows shot up in surprise. But I just smiled and jerked my head over at the bed. "You're the nice one." I winked.

It was true. I'd have trouble holding back. I wanted nothing more than to throw Ruby's feet up over my shoulders and rail her hard. But that wouldn't be good for her first time. And I didn't want to do anything to mess this up.

Migs slid off the bed and Bar climbed up on it next to her self-consciously.

"Hi," he said.

I wanted to face palm on his behalf, but I resisted.

Ruby didn't seem to notice the awkwardness because she reached right for his dick and started stroking, just like I'd taught her. "So, I know where this goes," she blinked up at him. "But you seem way too big."

She couldn't have said anything more right.

Bar lost his shy self-consciousness and rolled over to get in position on top of her. He kissed her hard as she continued to stroke him. Then he pulled back and used one hand to rub his dick up and down her slit. That made Ruby arch her back.

Fuuuuuck.

Those cherry nipples jiggled.

Bar said the last thing in the world I expected. "Guys? Can you help with her wings and nipples?"

Migs and I scrambled over to the other side of the bed. He took middle, since he hadn't gotten to play with those delicious breasts yet. I slid behind her and propped her upper torso on my lap, so that my hands could stroke the tops of those glorious wings. The feathers felt so soft against my skin. Wherever they rubbed felt hyper-sensitized afterword, the nerves tingling with pleasure.

Bar gently started to push into Ruby, which made her squirm. That made her wings rub against my dick. And fuck me! Sensation shot straight up my spine. I grew mindless as pleasure blazed a trail through me. It felt like pure white light was filling me up. Like choirs of naughty angels were singing and the vibrations of their song were running right along my dick. Fucking hell. Her wings weren't just regular wings. They were heaven's wings. Filled with every fucking delight imaginable. And when they touched my dick that delight shot right through it.

Bar stroked into Ruby and her wings brushed against me again.

She cried out gently and so did I.

"Bar!" she murmured.

"Ruby, your wings!" I groaned.

"What about the wings?" Migs asked.

But I couldn't open my eyes. I couldn't see straight. Her feathers brushed past my dick again as Bar moved faster and faster. The sensation on my dick intensified. My hands fell to the mattress as her wings continued to move. "Fuck, Ruby! Your wings!"

I felt the bed shift beside me and Migs ended up right next to me. He glanced over at my dick and saw how Ruby's feathers were running up and down the shaft.

"I don't think I can—" I gritted my teeth and tried to hold off.

Migs slid down next to me and I saw him thrust his dick into a patch of feathers.

"Aiiii!" he cried, pumping his hips up.

Bar leaned forward and started thrusting harder into Ruby.

We all seemed to cry out, "Yes!" at once. And my dick spasmed like it never had before. The orgasm made me see pure white, overtaking my vision as every part of my body writhed in bliss.

When my high ended and I came back down, my face turned to the side.

Migs had the same blissed out expression that I imagined I had.

I glanced down to check on Ruby and her plump lips were curved up in a smile. "I like mating," she murmured.

I looked up at Bar, who had pulled back almost instantly after coming. He was swiping at his face.

"Dude, is something wrong?" I asked.

"You both fucking jizzed on me!" He shouted.

My hand flew to my mouth and I had to clamp down on a surprised laugh.

Next to me, Migs couldn't hide his snort of laughter as he said, "Sorry, dude. We didn't know it was gonna happen. But next time, I'll totally take the facial. You gotta try Ruby's wings." He stroked her feathers affectionately, which caused her to curl up into him.

Wanting in on that action, I slid down a bit, so I could spoon her from behind. "Yeah, I'll take facials anytime you want to give them to me."

I laughed when Bar smacked me on the shoulder, just like I expected him to.

But I was surprised when he laid back down on top of Ruby, careful not to squish her, but cuddling her from above. I was surprised because he was touching us as well when he did so. But Bar didn't seem to notice that as he pressed a gentle kiss to Ruby's forehead. "I hope it was good for you, my warrior princess."

Ruby smiled. "Of course, it was. Can mating be bad?"

"If you have the wrong mate," Migs responded.

She giggled. "Oh, I definitely don't. God gave me just the perfect soulmates."

"Hell yeah he did," I said, snuggling into Ruby and inhaling her delicious cinnamon roll scent.

Post-sex snuggling brought out the philosopher in me. I realized that for the first time in a millennium, I felt like I was in exactly the right place at exactly the right time. I wasn't a demon trying to fly under the radar, discontent with his work and just killing time. I was Parker. Ruby's soulmate. I'd never in a million years thought I'd end up soulmates with an angel. I'd never in a million years thought that someone bad could end up with something this good.

I could burst into flames at any moment. If I did somehow cease to exist, I'd die happy. Because now I knew why I was here.

To help her.

To love her.

AFTERWORD

Thank you so much for reading about Ruby and her guys!!!

Thank you from the bottom of my heart for supporting my dream of constructing beautiful worlds with words. If you liked this book, please leave an Amazon review. It's how indie authors like myself make it into the algorithms at Amazon so other readers can find us. Plus, your reviews keep me motivated.

XOXO!

There's info about more books, my newsletter, this series, and my Facebook group on the following pages.

READ OTHER JEWELS CAFE BOOKS

If you liked Ruby, you'll enjoy these other Jewels Cafe books:

Amber by Mia Harlan
Sapphire by Eva Delaney
Peridot by M Sinclair Author
Opal by Candace Wondrak
Topaz by J.E. Cluney
Ruby by Ann Denton
Amethyst by CY Jones
Pearl by Tabitha Barret
Emerald by Jade Waltz
Onyx by Melissa Adams
Moonstone by Lucy Felthouse
Rose by Jewels Arthur

Flip the page to read a preview of AMETHYST by CY Jones!

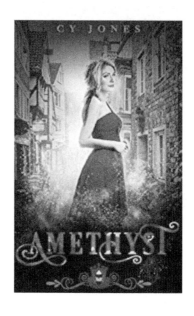

BLURB

Amethyst is a curse worker on the run after hexing her ex. (He he that rhymes) On the bus to Silver Springs, she meets a set of hot twins but with a vengeful ex after her and a group of pissed off vampires, she's a little distracted. In a town she swore she would never return to she runs into her old tormentor, a hot af wolf shifter, befriends an angel, and spends more time ducking and dodging her family members than she would like. Lady Luck is supposed to be on her side, but with so many problems, what's a girl to do? Maybe a pumpkin spiced drink and 3 hotter than hell supernaturals is just what Amethyst needs, or will her hatred over her past keep her from opening her heart and have her end up hexing herself.

CHAPTER 1 PREVIEW

ON THE RUN

When the arrival of my bus is announced, I stand and take a hesitant step towards the loading dock. I can't believe I'm about to board a bus and leave sunny NOLA to go back home to freeze your lady balls off in New York. Back to the small town of Silver Springs where I grew-up. A place I vowed to never return to again, but fate had other plans for me, and in my current situation, my choices are limited. As in, I have none and Silver Springs is my best bet for survival. Resigned to my fate, I gather the duffle bag filled with what's left of my old life and walk with my shoulders back and head held high towards the loading dock. After handing my bag over to the driver to load, I take a seat in the back, scooting all the way to the window. I slide my leg across the empty seat, preventing anyone from sitting next to me. I don't want to end up with some friendly vacationers trying to chat me up during the 13 hours it will take to get to New York, that's including the four stops in between. Logically, I know from here to there someone will end up sitting by me, but for now, the bus still has plenty of empty seats for me to get away with my antisocial behavior. Just for good measure, I put on my perfected resting bitch face, scaring away anyone brave enough to consider sitting by me.

Once the driver steps back onto the bus and starts the engine, I sigh in both relief and dread. I'm relieved I got away, but I dread where I'm going. I know what you're thinking. If I hate my hometown so much, then why am I going back? To answer that question, I need to start from the beginning. I'm a witch. Yes, you heard me right. I'm a real witch and not the kind that starts with a B. Witches really do exist, as well as other supernaturals, but we're talking about me right now.

As the bus pulls away, I duck down when I notice the flaming red hair of my ex. It could be my imagination, but I swear as the bus drives by, his bright green eyes are staring lasers into the side of the bus where I am currently seated, but that's impossible right? If anything, I know luck. Part of my witch powers is that Lady Luck is always on my side. What does that mean? It means I'm lucky as shit. It's the only magic I got from my mother. My other magic is the reason why I don't want to go back home. The coven I'm from is made up of good witches, or light witches as they're now called. Think Glinda, the good witch of Emerald City. The problem is the majority of my magic comes from my father, who definitely was not a good witch, and hadn't come from a light witch family. He's powerful, with very strong hex and karma magic, and was the reason I was able to hex my ex. Hah, that rhymes. Sorry, I'm losing focus again. So what do you get when Glinda and a powerful karma mage bump uglies and make a baby? You get me, a powerful curse maker with a touch of Lady Luck, 'ta da.' Please hold your applause for the end.

That sounds awesome, doesn't it? Well, it's really not. It sucks balls because my family hates me. When I was nothing but a little pineapple living in my mom's tummy, her mother and the other witches in her coven banished my father, running him out of town, which is pretty hypocritical seeing how they're supposed to be the good guys. As a result, my mother fell into a deep depression and had me prematurely. She was never able to break free from the depression, and mere hours after my birth she died of, what I think was, a broken heart. I was given to my aunt, my mom's younger sister, and grandmother to raise. While growing up, it didn't take long for everyone to tell I was different. I was never the happy go lucky kid my coven wanted me to be. Spreading joy and laughter like a bunch of hippies was never my thing. I hated school and almost failed. The academy I went to is one of the two schools most of the supes in New York go to instead of junior high and high school. It took a very perceptive mage to figure out I wasn't a good witch at all. I can't do all those goodie two shoe spells. I don't hold the power or capability for it, but hexing and cursing people, well, that's my jam. I can work the dark arts like a pro. If this was a Harry Potter movie, I would totally be placed in Slytherin by the Sorting Hat. I'm a beast, and as a result, one of the most powerful hexers in the world, much to my family's horror.

To them, I'm like the stain on the carpet you try to cover up when company comes over, except they smothered me and hid me my whole life. If it weren't for the mage at the academy, I would have never learned the extent of my powers and would have been no more powerful than a human. My family was more willing to let my magic die than admit I wasn't like them. You tell me, who is the bad guy in this story? As soon as I turned 18 and graduated, I left town and never looked back. Now that I'm older and looking back now, 18 was way too young to venture out into the real world alone. I was young and naïve, and as soon as I arrived in New Orleans, I fell hard for the wrong supernatural. Cliche, I know.

Available Now on Amazon!

ACKNOWLEDGMENTS

A huge thanks to Rob, Rachel, Thais, Elle, Mia, Raven and Ivy. Thanks to my cover designer, J.E. Cluney, and my amazing ARC readers.

MORE BOOKS

Tangled Crowns Series

Knightfall - Book 1

MidKnight - Book 2

Knight's End - Book 3

My second reverse harem series is the Lotto Love series. Its a rom-com reverse harem with a private island, lottery money, and tons of handsome men.

Lotto Love Series

Lotto Men - Book 1

Lotto Trouble - Book 2

If you liked the sense of humor in this story, you might want to check out my Urban Fantasy mysteries. They are silly and snarky and full of laughs with a slow burn romance.

The Lyon Fox Mysteries

Magical Murder

Enchanted Execution

Supernatural Sleep

Hexed Hit

If you're in the mood for more intrigue, check out my Postapocalyptic Thriller series.

Timebend

Melt

Burn

CONNECT AND GET SNEAK PEEKS

If you would like to read exclusive snippets from different characters, make predictions with other readers, see my inspiration for books, or just come hang and be yourself, I have a Facebook reader group full of amazing people.

Feel free to join Ann Denton's Reader Group.

ABOUT ME

I have two of the world's cutest children, a crazy dog, and an amazing husband that I drive somewhat insane as I stop in the middle of the hallway, halfway through putting laundry away, picturing a scene.

Printed in Great Britain
by Amazon

30501166R00136